IT'S ABOUT TIME

B. A. DILLON

Edited by Dawn Waltuck
Cover Design by Airicka Phoenix
Cover Copyright © Airicka's Mystical Creations,
www.AirickaPhoenix.com
Formatting: Champagne Formats

ISBN-13:978-1517708436
ISBN-10:1517708435

DEDICATION

For anyone who believes in love <3

CHAPTER ONE

Scott

Born This Way

MARRIAGE.
A civil, social and legal institution under which two consenting adults establish a life-long relationship based on love and commitment.

As of today, I'm unable to enter into this arrangement with the man I love.

The reason. I am gay man living in the state of Florida.

The realization that I was gay boiled to the surface multiple times while I was growing up. I ignored it, pushed it down and denied it every time. But there was one moment, a life-altering evening, that all my ignored emotions bubbled to the surface like a full eruption on Mount Vesuvius.

All gay people come out . . . eventually. It's just a question of when and where and with whom. Homosexuality is a sensitive and controversial subject, and when one comes out it is typically painful, lengthy and difficult for everyone. Especially mothers. My mom struggled. A lot. But I find solace in the fact that I came out and moved through this entire experience whole and unmarked. It took my family awhile to accept who I am, but eventually we all mended whatever fences fell.

As a kid, I knew I was different. While most kids go through awkward, gangly, and sometimes ugly stages, I knew I was different in a different way. I never suffered from lack of confidence – I knew I was fabulous from the word GO. But I never flaunted my style. I always had a gaggle of friends or people to hang with and seemed to find my niche in music and food very early in life. Thank God for food. My grandmother discovered my love for the kitchen and convinced my parents I had a gift. Cooking kept me sane and believe it or not kept people from asking too many questions. They were too busy eating whatever magnificent creation I put before them.

My life was a breeze in one department because the gene pool did its thing. My parents still are a striking couple. Both my brother and I inherited rich royal blue eyes from my mother's side of the family, and thick, dark-blonde hair from my dad's side. Girls loved us both and I was told on more than one occasion that with my eyes I looked like a blonde Chris Pine. My brother took the time to build his body and he still looks as tough as he fights. I love to run and make a point to let my feet pound the pavement every morning. Even in the rain. That's why my legs are my best feature. Not my eyes. My entire family has always worked hard to stay in shape. We had to. I was always cooking up something super delicious in the kitchen – a meal that could easily add ten pounds.

Growing up in my small Mississippi town, I didn't have to pretend to be like all the other kids because I truly acted like most kids. I didn't like to play team sports, but I became a loud and obnoxious football fan early in life. I knew the game inside-out, and could be a part of any conversation that included football stats. My dad loved that about me. Football Sundays consisted of me whipping up our favorite football snacks, my brother devouring every morsel and then watching the game next to the two most important guys in my life. This was our special time and why my brother and I are so close.

To please my mother, I did very well in school. I was the straight "A" kid my entire life, and didn't earn my first "B" until college. For the record, there was only one. That damn "B" will haunt me for the rest of my life.

Like all good families in Lakewood, Mississippi my family spent every Sunday morning and evening in church. According to the choir director at Southside Baptist, I had the voice of an angel. I was the 'S' in ACTS, a small choral group, built entirely around talent and friendship and we sang every Sunday. Anthony, 'A', my older brother by just eleven months, also sang and played the piano. His best friend, Aiden, picked up the guitar at age five, and never put it back down. Sean sang the lead on every song we performed, and we were all certain he'd end up on American Idol someday. Tyler, Connor, and Chris rounded out the group and added to our rich four-part harmony. The seven of us were extraordinarily tight. No one messed with any of us for fear they'd have to deal with the other six. We spent nearly every waking moment together through middle and high school. All of us, including me, always had a girl on our arm. Most of the guys had them in their beds as well. Even I traveled down that path a few times, but realized very early, the lady vajayjay was not for me.

In addition to church, our school got ahold of us and we all dove headfirst into a very active musical theater program. I had a leading role in every musical production the school developed including *Grease, Lil' Abner, and Oklahoma*. Yeah, I know . . . very stereotypically gay. But because we **all** loved it, the entire community supported the boys of ACTS, and no one ever suggested any of us were gay.

Anthony, Aiden, Connor, Tyler and Sean were most definitely NOT gay. Their escapades all through school, and my association with them, kept the gay radar from zeroing in on me. Instead, the entire population in my small Mississippi town believed we were all headed for stardom. No one questioned our sexual orientation. Which is why everyone, even me at one point, overlooked what was happening. I don't remember all the details of how it began, but during my junior year of high school, I accepted one fact as my guiding principle. Me and Chris . . . were most definitely gay.

One night after a party, Chris offered me a ride home.

We openly flirted the entire drive and I'm surprised we made it home in one piece. Although our touching was unbalanced and rough, I was completely turned on and ready to explore my sexuality. I didn't even try to hide the growing evidence pushing against my jeans, and neither did he. I made it very clear I liked him more than friendship allowed, and Chris didn't seem bothered by it in the slightest. I don't remember how it happened, but somehow I ended up spending the night at his house. With his parents out for the evening, my time with Chris was the first time in my whole life that I was completely *me* in front of another human being. It was the first time I kissed a guy, stood naked in front of a guy, touched another guy, and experienced sensuality.

For the first time in my life, a kiss felt romantic. Sex felt the way I imagined it was always supposed to feel. I actually understood the meaning behind all the lyrics of the love songs we sang together as a group. I actually felt those emotions, even though I wasn't at all sure what to do with them. That night was the first time I ever allowed myself to consider, for just one moment, that I could be with a guy for my entire life. That moment would define who I was and who I would become. The night I had my first sexual encounter with Chris took place nearly one year after my last heterosexual experience, and I never traveled the hetero path again.

Our relationship continued quietly all through high school. Chris and I never talked about what was happening, but we had sex almost every weekend for nearly two years.

To blend in, we both dated a lot and took girls to our senior prom. For some reason, Chris stayed wrapped up in his prom date through the entire summer. Then he went away to college. Far away. I haven't talked to him in nearly ten years, but I remember Chris. My first encounter with him is etched into my memory forever. I remember every nuance of how I felt before, during, and after that moment – and it changed me forever.

Chris gave me the courage to be my true self. Chris gave me the will to be fabulous. Chris allowed me to come out of the closet to find real love. And once that door was open, I found real love with the man of my dreams, Brandon Lawrence.

CHAPTER TWO

Scott

Marry Me

66**T**HE LAST OF your personal stuff is loaded in the car. The truck already left and we're supposed to meet Sierra in the Fiesta Rentals parking lot. If we don't hurry up, they're gonna be closed and you, my love, will lose your deposit and today's adventure will set you back a week's pay." When I look over at Brandon I know he's recognized my emotional turmoil and that one of my schizophrenic moods is about to make an appearance. Emma and Luke just said *I Do* on Honeymoon Island and like always, Amuse Bouche, my new catering venture with my cousin Sierra, delivered a beautiful meal on the beach for the happy couple. The ceremony has left me almost lifeless but happy that my new start-up created a magical event for my good friends. I'm caught somewhere between touched and delighted, bewildered and confused, and blissfully cranky. Three minutes ago when the sunlight touched the warm gulf waters, I decided tonight was the night.

"I'm standing here admiring the view and feeling a little sorry for myself. I just need a couple of minutes."

When the words fall from my lips I know I'm opening a can of worms Brandon Lawrence will never allow me to ignore. Inching in, he towers over me ready to talk me out of my mood. He looks scrumptious today – completely edible. And I have to wonder how I landed this perfect man. Perfect chestnut hair, perfect chocolate brown eyes, and perfect dark scruff. I love the feel of that scruff when he kisses me every morning. He claims his lips are too thin and without color, but I think they're perfect especially when they cover mine. Even the space between his two front teeth is adorable. He hates that space and refuses an open mouth smile any time a camera a near. Even though he's older than me, he looks younger. And it's all because of that smile – when he shares that gap between his teeth. I call it his schoolboy smile.

Lifting my chin with his soft and manicured hand, I'm ready for his courtroom voice completely smothered in love. "Babe, what's wrong? Please don't question any of the choices you made for today. You did such a remarkable job giving Luke and Emma exactly what they asked for. This was the most relaxed wedding I've ever attended. Keeping it simple and allowing the small crowd to enjoy the beach was genius. Everyone wondered how you'd serve food on the sand. They couldn't stop talking about your wedding picnic baskets. And the food? Let me see if I remember all the details." Brandon lifts up his brown eyes and cradles his perfectly dimpled chin in a gesture of mock concentration. "Emma and Luke's guests began their experience with pepper crusted beef tenderloin, sliced, and served on a crispy baguette, spread with a horseradish mayo and coarse grain mustard, paired with mesclun greens. Even though some of the guys weren't sure what mesclun greens were, they ate it anyway. Every last delicious bite. Emma and Luke's picnic basket and beach blanket gift to each family was an incredibly sweet gesture. That was probably your idea, too. Right?" He asks while I nod confirming his suspicions. "I'm so proud of you, Scott. You refused to give up, and you work so hard. You made your dream a reality." When I feel his thumb reach up to trace lightly over my bottom lip, I can't hold back any longer.

"I love you," I whisper feeling tears wanting to escape my eyes. "I'm so jealous of all of them, and I feel like the world's worst friend because I'm thinking that way. I love Emma to death, and I'm so happy she found Luke and has a second chance at love. But with Shane and Katie expecting a baby and the romance that Mia and Isaac think they're hiding from the world, I just feel cheated. When do we get our happily ever after?" As soon as it's all out, I feel like shit for saying anything. Gay marriage is legal in almost half the country now, but still not here. My state still bans me from legally binding my life with Brandon. I want marriage and kids and a mortgage we can't afford. I'm a traditionalist . . . but I'm gay. And in Florida that means I can't marry the love of my life.

"Scott," he pauses covering my lips with his. One long kiss that invades my brain completely chases away my sour mood. "I'm already living my happily ever after with you. We've made a life together, a perfect life. But I'll jump a plane to Massachusetts tomorrow if that's what it takes to make you happy. In my heart, we're already joined forever. I love you."

I'm so caught up in the moment, I have no thoughts other than him . . . me . . . marriage. The moment is perfect. Grabbing Brandon's hand I pull him with me as I race to the water's edge. The sun has set, but the night sky is crystal clear and blanketed with twinkling lights from thousands of stars. The moon is full and blends shadows with the darkness that creates a mood so rich with romance I truly want to get married right here – right now. I don't care that Sierra is waiting for me in the Fiesta Rentals parking lot, wondering if I shanghaied the picnic table and 100 tiki torches. I don't care that I'm about to lower to one knee in my very new and very expensive Tommy Bahama linen pants. The salty ocean water is surely going to destroy my new Sperrys, but I don't care. I don't care that Brandon is trying to hurry me along. When did he become the responsible guy and we transition roles? All I know is that I want that promise. His promise of forever. When I kneel in front of him, he smiles large and laughs as I express momentary concern over the demise of my new linen pants and brand new Sperrys.

"Brandon Lawrence, I love you. And I want to make all your dreams come true. I want marriage and kids and a dream kitchen in the biggest house we can afford. As soon as it's legal in Florida, will you marry me?"

"Do you realize what you've just done to your shoes, Scott? I mean, we're wearing brand new $160 Sperrys, man!" Dropping to the sand with me, I'm treated to a kiss that rocks my world. "And, of course I'll marry you. We don't have to wait for Florida, Scott. I meant what I said. I'll get on a plane tomorrow if that's what it takes to convince you. I want to grow old with you. I want you to believe we'll have all that and more."

Rising from the rippling waters of the Florida Gulf, I pull Brandon into my body and mumble I love you a thousand times while kissing every inch of his beautiful face. My phone has buzzed about twenty times in the last hour. Probably Sierra wanting to skin me alive. Hopefully, she used the family charm and delivered a little white lie or two to score us an extension on the rentals. With our hands intertwined, we walk in comfortable silence to Brandon's car and prepare to race back to town. Laughing, we both remove our now soaked designer footwear. I can't help but wince as I place our ruined designer shoes in the trunk. Before we can pull out of the parking lot, Brandon pulls my hand to his lips, lingering for some time. His brows are furrowed, as his eyes skate back and forth over my left hand. "What's on your mind, honey? Cause if you're thinking about celebrating, so am I! But Sierra will use her expert slicing skills, dicing me into a million pieces if I'm not there to smooth things over with Fiesta Rentals first. But know I'm gonna rock your world in about an hour," I mention slyly while studying his serious expression.

"I was just imagining what this hand will look like after I put a ring on this finger," he murmurs while leaving one last kiss on the finger that will soon be wrapped in something truly stunning. "And I was also thinking that you better never drag me into the ocean water again wearing a new pair of Tommy Bahama linens and brand new Sperrys. Babe, your proposal was beautiful . . . but I think that little escapade in the salt water just set us back several hundred dollars."

Leaning in and offering him one last kiss, my smug smile gives everything away. "I'll remember that moment forever, honey, so it was worth every cent."

CHAPTER THREE

Scott

The Reason

A New Year. A New Promise.

"OKAY, DUDE! WHAT'S in or on this ham? I can't stop eating it!" Isaac bellows while filling his plate once again. "Damn, did you marinate it in crack or something? I ate about a pound of it at last night's party, and then you bring it back today?"

Laughing I can't keep my eyes off my good friend, Mia, and her man, Isaac Miller. It's hard to believe that less than six months ago Mia and Isaac were on the outs. But watching them tonight, I have to wonder if Isaac will be dropping down to one knee and popping 'the question' soon. They've been glued at the hip since August when school started.

Every time I see them together I'm almost winded by how much love washes over them.

The best part of tonight? Mia let me in on a GREAT BIG SECRET. Charlie, Luke's dad, is planning a New Year's Day proposal. Charlie fell head over heels in love with Mia's mom, Abby, this past summer and fall. Abby is blind, but she 'sees' more than all of us, and found Charlie in that blinding storm. I love this happily ever after moment. For months I really worried about Mia and her family, but it appears that both Mia and her mom are living a fairytale complete with another happily ever after moment.

But as happy as I am for all of them, I can't help feeling a bit cheated once again. Luke and Emma make marriage look easy. Katie and Shane are incredibly blessed with the arrival of their new baby girl, Lucy. Mia finally dropped her shields and allowed Isaac to sweep her off her feet. They have become a family with her two girls almost overnight. And now, even the old man, Charlie Myers, will have his happily ever after, too. Only Julia knows I proposed to Brandon after Emma and Luke's wedding. There's been so much going on the past few months, I asked her to keep my secret. Every time our group gathers together, someone has an announcement that I don't want to overshadow. Who am I kidding? I want a moment all for myself! And I'm convinced our news should wait until there's a good reason to celebrate.

Julia seems a bit quiet tonight, looking at Isaac's brother, Josh, like she could eat him for dinner. Ten bucks says she had a great New Year's Eve and had Josh in her bed last night. Brandon catches me stalking Julia and her prey and cocks his head to the left when my smile sours. With three strides he's at my side and I'm reminded why he's the love of my life. A chaste kiss. His school-boy smile. And his arms around me when my going gets tough. You see, he gets me and only wants me happy. Without a doubt Brandon loves me like no one else can, proving I waited for the right man. Caught up in our brief but idyllic moment my smile returns.

"Emma! We need music, woman!" Brandon hollers. Almost like magic, Emma cranks up the tunes and we are surrounded by my best girls. Mia, Emma, Rebecca, Katie and Julia's heels fly off their feet and for the next thirty minutes I shake my booty like tomorrow's never gonna come.

When the music slows, Brandon pulls me into a tight grip and leaves a tender, but all too brief kiss, very near my pouting lips. "Did you forget this is a party, bud? What's with the sad, puppy-dog face?" He asks while tipping my chin upward so I have to stare straight into his chocolate brown eyes. He looks incredible tonight. I love it when we dress down and comfortable. My man can truly rock a pair of True Religion jeans and a simple John Varvatos t-shirt. When it comes to the two of us, style is never an issue.

"I didn't forget it's a party. I'm so happy for all my friends. I really am. It's just I still want what they have. I'm jealous, and I have no problem saying that out loud. I keep checking my phone waiting for the news. Do you think . . . is there a chance?" Fearing the worst possible answer, I rest my head on Brandon's shoulder almost afraid to make eye contact. I love that Brandon is taller than me and that I fit so well in his arms.

When I finally dare to look up, I'm greeted by a serious presence. Brandon wears only two expressions – deliberate and schoolboy. I treasure the funny man but appreciate his intelligence. When my man needs to make his presence known, he does so with such a savvy intellect, the average man cowers.

"Unless something out of the ordinary happens, there's more than a chance. The law is clear. The United States Supreme Court denied the state of Florida's request to extend the stay." That's his business side telling me he knows what he's talking about and to stop worrying. "Meaning you and I will be able to get a marriage license on January 5th – that's Thursday. Want to get married right after we get the license?" That's nonsensical Brandon wanting to play.

"Absolutely not!" My expression is guarded, and almost appalled that he would even suggest such nonsense.

"Okay. Not the response I expected," he whispers almost sounding concerned.

"Brandon Lawrence! Do you know me? I want a wedding. A big, over-the-top ceremony, with everyone I know and love in attendance. I want hydrangeas on the tables, rose petals on every square inch of the ceremony venue, and good Southern cooking. I want Mia's little girls in the frilliest flower girl dresses I can find, and you and I, sir, will be decked to the nines. I have a color scheme, a menu, a location, centerpieces, and your ring already picked out. My mother and I have been planning our wedding since the moment you and I bought the condo together. Brandon Lawrence, like all good Southern families, I have a wedding

16

fund," I announce with pride.

"Don't you mean, WE have a wedding fund? Do I get to pick anything? I already have your wedding ring."

"You can have anything you want, so long as it goes with everything I've already decided. We'll need to get the moms together soon, so they can – what did you just say?" Oh. My. God. I love this man. I seriously want to jump him right now.

"I said I already have your ring. Are you ever gonna share our big news with Emma, Mia and the rest of the gang? Oh! Wow! Mia and Isaac really need to get a room. I think she just put her hand on—"

"Stop watching them you idiot and kiss me! We're out of here right after Emma serves dessert." While wrapped up in the arms of my love I notice everyone looks completely exhausted. I'm sure Emma and Luke would probably like their house back. Between Christmas and New Year's, Emma has hosted the entire crew at least five times. I think Luke, Isaac and the rest of the guys had to work all day sorting out their latest case, so it looks as though they're ready to get their women home as well. Whispering for only Brandon ears, I plan our great escape and evening celebration. "I don't think we found our bed until the wee hours of the morning. I need eight uninterrupted hours with you, Brandon Lawrence. I have ideas of things we can do to celebrate the news later. We've got a date to set. Then I'm getting down on my knees again. Since you already said yes, there's no need for another proposal tonight. But you, sir, will see stars once again!"

CHAPTER FOUR

Scott

It's Your Love

"**S**ERIOUSLY, CUZ, YOUR friends are really good for business. How you managed to create such a magical event in just three days is beyond me. I can cook, but pulling this together on such short notice makes me want to bow to your greatness and kiss your feet." Sierra declares while helping me finish arranging the three cupcake flavors on my small, three-tiered stand. Irish Car-Bomb Red Velvet for Mia. My ten layer chocolate cake in cupcake form for Isaac, and Vanilla Bean for Sarah and Sophie. "And, by the way, I love the color coded cupcake wrappers to identify the three flavors, Scott. The framed cupcake key is genius."

"Listen, I just handled the food, and cooking for sixteen is a breeze. I couldn't have done it without you, Sierra." Charlie's lanai looks like it belongs on the cover of Bride Magazine. After only one very brief meeting with Mia and Isaac, my cousin found a way to light up Charlie Myer's porch and backyard for Mia and Isaac's nuptials. Gardenias and white candles are everywhere. Considering gardenias don't normally bloom in Florida for another four months made Sierra's quest to have Mia's favorite flowers front and center a difficult task. But once again my cousin is a genius at party décor and space planning. Twinkling lights line the pool cage, a Jason Mraz song flows through the sound system, and the crowd is over-the-moon happy. That's all that matters. And full bellies, too . . . that also matters.

"Still . . . you can cook. I'm glad we went with family style and allowed the troops to serve themselves. I doubt we could have found servers at the last minute anyway. But you hit it out of the park with the lamb. I know Isaac and Mia wanted an intimate family affair, but you seriously classed up the menu. I'm glad Abby suggested lamb. The ladies are in heaven, and the guys and kids have no idea what they ate – only that it is delicious. By the way, the oven-roasted Dijon and herb crusted rack of lamb melted in my mouth. Pairing that with Herbs de Provence potato gratin and the balsamic and parmesan roasted brussels sprouts sealed the deal. I heard Isaac tell Sophie he wasn't fond of sprouts but loved your concoction. Every plate looks like they are licked clean!"

I was simply shell-shocked when Mia and Isaac announced they wanted to get married in a week. The pure

hell they endured right after our superb New Year's Eve party and delicious New Year's Day good luck meal was right
out of Hollywood. The FBI's human trafficking case spiraled
out of control quick putting Mia and Isaac in the middle of
a true firestorm. But Mia has some pretty strong lady balls,
and Isaac's planned proposal in the Georgia Mountains
didn't surprise anyone.

I'm not sure if we knew what to say or do when they
announced they wanted to marry the very next Saturday.
Everyone was truly speechless – for about three minutes.
But Isaac demanded something magical for 'his girls' and
said he'd pay top dollar if I could make it happen. All of us
– Mia, Emma, Julia, Rebecca, Katie and I took three days
off right after the winter break to help make Mia's dream
wedding come true. Our principal wasn't thrilled by our
absences, but our colleagues stepped up and helped cover
our classes whenever a substitute teacher wasn't available.
During those three days Sierra and I pulled it all together.
Isaac insisted on covering my lost salary, in addition to the
very handsome fee he agreed to pay to make Mia's dream
ceremony come true.

Once again, my news . . . our news took a back seat.
With the exception of Julia, the rest of our friends are unaware of our pending nuptials. I quietly began planning
our ceremony, selecting invitations and Brandon's and my
wardrobe. Brandon and I set of date near my dad's birthday
by confirming April 17th with both sets of parents. I immediately went into party planning mode with my mother. I
always wanted outdoors and rustic. That's been my dream.

So when Sierra performed her typical party planning magic by securing the Terrail Ranch for the ceremony, I was over-the-moon excited. The Wilson-Lawrence wedding will be a first for the Terrail Ranch – the first LEGAL gay wedding in the venue's history. But one sour note still plays constantly – our plan lacks luster because outside of our families, our friends are still in the dark. Or so I think.

Once the cupcakes are proudly on display, and the guests are dancing, I leave the clean up to Sierra and join Brandon at the table. As I look out over this unbelievably close-knit group, I feel incredibly blessed. With all the re-ferrals, my friends have seriously turned my new catering venture with Sierra into an overnight success. Just the book-ings from this crowd alone is a great start. But I also learned a thing or two while planning Emma and Mia's weddings. I found I truly loved shaping these intimate affairs. Charlie and Abby's wedding will be next, and Isaac mentioned host-ing another party two weeks after their ceremony. Evidently, he petitioned the courts just yesterday to legally adopt Mia's daughters, Sarah and Sophie. I love these people. I need to share my happy news with them. I'll have everyone over for breakfast next Saturday. That's a great plan. But before I can put a word out to have a private convo with my best girls inside, Isaac stands to make yet another toast. These people . . . way overdo the toasts.

"I promise, this is the last speech. I know I said that earlier, but I have a lot to say today. I'm not sure if I have the right words to express what today means to me . . . to Mia . . . to our girls . . . to our family, except that we are so happy we are able to share this day with all of you. I'm grateful for so much, but especially for this family we've managed to piece together. So, I was a little bit saddened when our resident big-mouth – that would be Julia for those of you not paying attention – let me in on a little secret our pal, Scott, has been keeping from the rest of us." Isaac turns toward me and continues, "Scott, you manage to kick every family event up a notch. The food tonight . . . there are no words, and no leftovers. Somehow you made Emma and Luke's wedding, Mia's birthday, parties galore and now this magical day for my family – exceptional. So tonight, I want everyone on this patio living the dream, bud. Anything you'd like to share?"

"Julia . . . what did you do?" I whisper across the table at my smiling friend.

"Secrets are hard to keep, Scott! And I've been hanging onto this one for quite some time. Just had a little slip of the tongue." Turning to Josh she mumbles, "All right big boy – what did you do?"

"Seriously, babe!" Josh bellows. "How was I supposed to know it was a secret? You never revealed that little tidbit. I just mentioned it in passing to Isaac earlier today. I thought he knew."

With turning heads flipping back and forth, along with the subtle whispers, Emma glances through the crowd and mentions with ease, "Anyone else feel lost here? Scott, what's going on?"

"Isaac, seriously, not the right time," I voice while refusing eye contact with anyone else.

"Scott, stop with the excuses. You'd think after all the

excitement that surrounded Emma and Luke's wedding, and our rush to tie the knot you would have learned a thing or two. There's never a right time. A perfect time. It's about making time for what really matters. All of us . . . we're your extended family, my friend, and we only want you and Brandon happy. Now tell these lovely ladies your news. Oh, and be prepared – they're gonna be a little pissed I knew before them."

Looking around the lanai, the faces of my closest friends come into view. Brandon grabs my hand under the table and gives it a little squeeze, encouraging me to break my silence. "I asked Brandon to marry me, and he said yes, of course," I whisper timidly. Brandon says when I'm embarrassed I look younger than my 28 years. Right now I'm slightly embarrassed and a little petrified of my best girls.

"Oh my God! That's such great news!" Mia screams while climbing from her chair and throwing her arms around my neck. "When did you ask him? Brandon, I want to hear all about his proposal! Have you set a date?"

"Mia, babe, maybe just one question at time," Isaac retorts while pulling Mia to his lap and placing a soft kiss at her temple. Seriously, what's with all the lap sitting? Hmmm . . . lap sitting. Now there's something we haven't done in a while.

"I asked Brandon at the beach after Emma and Luke's wedding last summer," I begin.

"You what?!" Not knowing where or who to look at first, I'm a little taken aback by the girls' combined general reaction. Somehow my news has shocked them into silence.

"I said I asked Brandon at the beach last summer – I . . ."

"So why is this the first time we're hearing the happy news, pal?" Emma questions solemnly.

"Ladies, the last year has been . . . eventful," I mention with a sly smile. "First, getting married wasn't an option for us until this year . . . this month. Second, I didn't want my news to overshadow all the good stuff happening for each of you. Third, it's only been legal in Florida for about three weeks, and we just set the date on New Year's Day. I hoped to share my news with you on Saturday. I planned on having you over for breakfast, but Isaac decided you all needed to know tonight. The intimate family thing suits all of you so well, but definitely not my style. Expect over 200 people at our ceremony, ladies. Remember, I'm a true Southern gentleman. I have lots of cousins and a wedding fund."

"So when are we getting you married, my friend?" Julia shouts with a raised glass. "And are we still invited for breakfast Saturday morning?"

"April 17th and yes, bring your appetites. Breakfast is at nine."

CHAPTER FIVE

Scott

You and Me

"**A**RE THERE ANY singles left in this crowd?" Sierra asks while laughing at her own question.

"Just Julia. Why?"

"So should we start planning her wedding now? The way these people like to get married on a moment's notice, she'll probably want to get hitched next month. She's with Josh, Isaac's brother. Right?"

Continuing to load my personal serving dishes in the car, I examine Charlie Myer's beautiful landscaping and home beaming with pride. Sierra and I just hit another homerun in the world series of party planning. Of all the family weddings this year, I think Charlie and Abby's was my favorite. Their love is so honest, so real, it just grabs you at the gut and refuses to let go. The love that surrounds this entire family is something truly spectacular. I know Brandon and I are rock solid just by watching my best girls and the guys that stole their hearts. Our love for one another is rooted just as deep as the love Abby and Charlie feel for each other. There's an ease that surrounds Emma and Luke – like they've known each other forever. Their hearts feel connected. And the way Isaac looks at Mia is so raw. It feels like she's the reason his heart beats every day. My relationship with Brandon mirrors all those emotions. Seventy-eight days and counting until I become Scott Wilson-Lawrence.

"Yeah, she's with Josh, but I wouldn't hold your breath. Julia never stays with anyone very long and Isaac's brother is kind of messed up," I mention wondering if I've said too much. The only down side today was Julia. It's almost like she's retreating inward, and pulling away from the land of the living. Note to self – talk to Emma about Julia's weird behavior tomorrow.

"You and Julia are friends? Like really close friends?"

"Yep. Why? Did something happen?"

"Today, well, she was, I'm not sure how to put this. She's weird, Scott. She talks to thin air, like all the time. I caught her having a full-blown convo with absolutely no one in the dining room. She didn't even flinch when she saw me watching her." Sierra's not typically the gossipy girl type so this has me even more concerned. Note to self – mention Sierra's observations to Emma first thing tomorrow. "I noticed she sort of strayed from Josh all day. Come to think about it, she didn't eat much. The entire family ate everything we served, but Julia just moved food around on her plate. Every time the family was ready for pictures they had to hunt her down in the bathroom."

"I wouldn't read too much into it. Julia is a loner. She's been with Josh for maybe five weeks now. In Julia time, that's like 75 years. They're probably just screwing like rabbits! But you are right about one thing, this family loves a great party. Both of Emma's kids are engaged and we should lock in their dates soon. I'm sure there are at least two more Myers-Miller family weddings for us to plan!"

"The Myers-Miller clan has certainly been great for business."

"Here-here! We have been hanging out with them a lot, huh? You have everything ready for the adoption party next Friday night?" I question while pushing my passenger side door closed.

"Yeah, Isaac didn't have any special requests this time – only to make it family friendly. But with Valentine's Day on Saturday, I'm going with a red and white theme. I also ordered a photo booth. Charlie is behind that grand gesture. There are a few surprises in the works as well. It seems Emma's daughter, Grace, never used any of her vacation days while serving in Africa, so she's being discharged from the Peace Corps one month early. Emma doesn't know she's coming home this weekend. Luke and her kids want to make this a big Valentine's Day surprise for her. Mia and Abby know Grace will be here, but I'm not sure if her fiancé, Ian is joining her. As far as the food goes, get your final number from Mia – not Isaac. These people are something else. I'm surprised Isaac didn't order a pony."

"Nope. No pony. But he's sticking with the adoption theme. He's filled out all the paperwork to adopt a puppy from the local rescue league. Mia doesn't even know. Emma's son KJ is bringing the puppy over Friday afternoon," I announce while laughing. "That puppy is going to pee on everything they own!"

It's after ten when I finally walk through our front door. I'm exhausted and there's no second wind coming tonight. The schedule I've been keeping the last few months has been a killer, but I am reaping the rewards as Amuse Bouche is growing by leaps and bounds. At some point I have to make a decision if I can continue to teach all day, cook at night, and be present at all the weekend events. I feel like I've only seen Brandon at a Myers-Miller event or when I crawl into bed next to him each night. I know I kissed him today – several times. But when was the last time I had my hands on him? I don't remember.

As I enter the foyer I hear the hum of the television, but the room is shaded in darkness. Only one side lamp, dimmed to its lowest wattage, offers any light. The kitchen is clean with the exception of the small plastic container resting on the counter that once held a small sliver of Abby and Charlie's wedding cake. Brandon had a ton of paperwork to do tonight so he left right after Abby and Charlie cut the cake. Ever since he made partner at the firm, his weekend work load has tripled.

Like almost every night, Brandon is kicked back on the couch, eyes closed, and snoring softly. He's still dressed except for his shoes, and his reading glasses are poised on his nose. A file folder full of papers rest near his stomach while two fingers still grasp one document tightly. He must have fallen asleep mid-read. His chestnut brown hair is still perfectly styled to perfection and he's promoting a silly grin. He must be dreaming. The beard or scruff he insists on sporting offers more depth to his chin. It seems darker at night, taking away from his normally angelic face. At first I just study his mouth, remembering last Sunday morning when he kneeled at my body and had those full lips firmly around my dick in the shower. Just looking at his mouth has me all kinds of ready for another round of shower sex, and that second wind I thought wasn't in my future is now screaming to come out and play.

As quietly as I can move, I find my way to Brandon's side and slip off his glasses. Capturing his mouth with mine, I kiss him with such urgency I forget to fill my lungs with enough air. Before he has a chance to react, I'm careful to remove the file folder, placing the contents of whatever he was studying on the center coffee table. "Hi," I breathe as I cover his mouth once again with a softer more sensual kiss that I feel everywhere. Simply everywhere. "I need you naked. Naked right now," I direct in an authoritative tone.

"Hello to you, too," he answers with a smiley yawn. I can't help but laugh as he nearly falls twice attempting to hastily remove his shirt, socks, pants and boxers in record time. Barely able to hold onto my load, my gaze travels the length of his body to his rip roaring hard-on. "I was dreaming about you. I thought you'd be ready to crash the minute you got home." With no chance to answer his question, Brandon rises up and off the couch in record time and is moving his tongue around my mouth with ease. I want it all tonight. I'm gonna have him seeing stars and then I'm putting him on all fours and taking complete control.

As soon as I'm able, I break contact and begin my descent. Nothing about the next hour can be rushed. I want to savor every minute and make him squirm with desire. Stopping to lavish over his nipples, I continue my journey over his taught belly, nipping at the skin as gently as I can before reaching the holy land. I try to keep my pace slow, only grazing slowly with my mouth while my hand works up and down his lubricated shaft. The deeper I can take my mouth the better. With a tight grip at the base of the shaft I feel Brandon's hand move into my hair and tug me in closer. Feverishly working my tongue, my lips, and my hand I can feel and hear Brandon's reaction to my movements and know he's closer than I want him to be at this moment. He wants faster right now, but I want longer and more tonight. I hope we don't sleep a wink. Removing my mouth suddenly I instruct Brandon's movements while beginning to remove my shirt. "Sit on the couch and slide to the edge."

At first he begins to question my assertive directions. I'm sure he's feeling the vacancy of my traveling tongue, but then thinks carefully knowing my mouth is going to have him erupting with joy soon. When I return to my knees I set a slow pace again for a few short minutes outlining my mouth with his cock, and flicking my tongue over the head. I notice immediately his breath picks up to short spurts as I hear him muttering words of enthusiasm. Gently my tongue picks up a regular rhythm as I lick the entire length from base to head, leaving us both so lubricated we'll be able to take what's left from this adventure back to the bedroom for more. When I see his toes begin to wiggle and his back arch high off the couch I know he's ready. Wanting to give him a moment he'll not soon forget, I give a quick tug to his balls right as my fingers begin their journey to his backside.

"Oh God, Scott! I can . . . I need to . . . can't form a coherent thought."

"Come here to me. Feel this?" I ask while wrapping my hand at the base of his neck forcing him to make direct eye contact. "This is what you do to me just laying on my couch. I'm taking you to bed tonight." Continuing to massage the remnants of our last adventure, my mouth captures his for the roughest kiss we've shared all night. Guiding him toward our bed, I utter the last full rational thought either of us will share for the next hour. "I'm making you mine in every possible way tonight. Never letting work get in the way of us again."

CHAPTER SIX

Scott

I Lived

I AM COMPLETELY EMOTIONALLY spent today.

This celebration . . . there are no words.

Well . . . maybe there are a few words.

Love. Love times a zillion. Love.

Today is Friday, February 13th, but there's no bad luck hanging around. At least not where this family is concerned. The day begins at the courthouse. Brandon handled all the legal mumbo jumbo for Mia and Isaac, moving the entire adoption proceeding through the system at lightning speed. The entire gang is front and center once again. I think our coworkers at Pride Middle School are just about done with all of us missing so many days. Emma talked our principal, Mr. McRae, down from his recent rant, reminding him of why all of us are so close in the first place. It began at work because of the family environment he promotes. Then she promised the big family events were coming to a close soon.

Even Emma's son, KJ, took the day off and drove over from Orlando. I love watching Luke and Charlie with all the kids. Especially the grown ones. Luke has a real friendship with KJ, and I love listening to Charlie offer his two cents on Tampa Bay Lightning hockey and the upcoming Rays baseball season. Both Luke and his dad are just incredible role models for everyone in this crowd.

My best girls have been nothing but waterworks all morning long. Even the judge handling the case has been wiping away tears. She continues to pause frequently in order to regain her composure, offering Mia and Isaac a reminder of how lucky they are to have this wonderful extended family standing with them. I am honored to be here. Even the tough cops are a little misty eyed as the judge begins asking Sarah and Sophie a few questions.

"Sarah, do you know why you're here today?" The judge inquires.

"Yes ma'am. So we can be adopted by Isaac," Sarah answers clearly.

"Do you want to be adopted, Sarah?" The judge asks for clarification.

"Yes I do," Sarah continues with ease.

"What does it mean to you to be adopted, Sarah?" The judge questions further.

"Sophie and I want the same last name as our mom and mostly because Isaac is already our dad in every way that matters. We're a family, ma'am. We all got married several weeks ago. We just all need the same last name, please. He's my dad in my heart." Sarah proclaims while beaming with pride.

The courtroom erupts with relaxed laughter and many sniffles as Sarah and Sophie confidently explain to the judge why she needs to sign the papers expeditiously. I cannot stop crying. Seriously. Blubbering like a fool.

I love watching Brandon work, but a part of me wishes he was next to me. As he begins to present Mia and Isaac with countless forms I notice even his sitting posture states 'I'm in charge, here.' He looks every bit the professional wearing an understated black suit and crisp white dress shirt paired with a red tie. But not me. This is a party today, and it is Valentine's Day tomorrow. I'm wearing the brightest red slacks I own and the boldest Valentine's Day tie I could find in my closet.

After signing a million pieces of paper the judge proclaims Sarah and Sophie will forever bear the Miller last name. It wasn't until the proceedings came to a close did I realize Sophie never left Isaac's lap. She kept her arm firmly locked around his neck almost as if she were afraid someone would take him away.

This day has been nothing but happy tears. Blissful, magical, happy tears. Someday soon Brandon and I will have a moment just like this one. I seriously cannot wait! I'm sure there's more blubbering to come. There are at least two more surprises in store for the family later today. A puppy and Emma's daughter's homecoming. While the family poses for pictures with the judge, I beeline it back to Mia and Isaac's home to help Sierra with the final preparations. Hopefully my dinner will only add to this momentous occasion.

Sierra insisted we run with family style again, but that left me with a small equipment nightmare. Between the two of us we decided to serve Italian. I knew I would be at the courthouse prior to today's dinner, so food preparation was a huge concern. Business is booming and with that Sierra and I decided four days ago we needed to update our serving equipment. We also decided we desperately needed a bigger vehicle to transport all of the food and necessities to our functions. On Wednesday night I picked up our brand new Toyota Highlander hybrid and eight new crockpots. This was Brandon's generous investment in Amuse Bouche. Once this function is over, Brandon and I have to have a serious discussion about our kitchen. Bottom line – it's not big enough to handle what I spend most nights doing. Cooking for parties of sixteen or more.

For this function, we're serving up an Italian feast to celebrate the guests of honor and the two name changes that were just formalized at the courthouse. Sarah Michelle James just became the extraordinary bright and beautiful Sarah Michelle Miller. And little Sophie Abigail James proudly announced to everyone that her name is now Sophie Abigail Miller. Brandon and I had several things designed and personalized for the girls by our friends at Thirty-One Bags. Our gifts include new lunch bags for school and small overnight bags for their many sleep-overs with Nana and Papa Charlie – each sporting their new initials.

God! I can't wait to have kids. And I need a little girl! Brandon and I want to adopt three children, as soon as possible. To expedite the process, one of the partners at Brandon's firm is representing us, and has some of the initial paperwork already complete. I'm getting married in sixty-three days, and I could be a dad as early as summer break. I need a bigger kitchen for business and we need a bigger home since we both want kids right away. Damn! I want a baby girl sooooooo bad!

I'm a little concerned for today's function. Mia and Isaac's home is a bit smaller than Charlie and Abby's place, so Sierra needs to be a space décor master. We're expecting 22 at today's party, and we've never served that many people at a Myers-Miller intimate affair. Last night we moved some of the extra furniture into the garage to make room for the tables. Since the weather is unusually cool for Tampa, we brought in a couple of propane outdoor heaters to make use of the lanai space. When I arrive I find Sierra calmly moving through the kitchen with ease, stopping to check each crockpot with a quick taste-test.

"Hey cuz! The family is probably an hour behind me. How's the Bolognese?"

"It's rich and robust. The pork and veal make this dish elegantly rustic. By adding the pappardelle pasta, the comfort factor is accentuated. Perfect for family style serving. You did it again, Scott. I have to admit, your menus are brilliant. Like all the time brilliant!"

"Thanks, Sierra," I mumble with muted enthusiasm.

"Okay . . . what's wrong?"

"Nothing," I answer quickly while prepping the pasta.

"Liar! Spill."

"I'm a little worried. I think I should have insisted we host this party at Charlie and Abby's."

"Scott, you know this business better than most. Which means you also know we have to go with what the client wants. They just officially became a family and needed this one at their own home."

"I know, but we've never served from crockpots before. We've never served this many people at an intimate family gathering before. And the space feels small and weird. And did I mention I blubbered all the way through the entire affair today. I'm tired and emotionally spent. I didn't know how much I needed this downtime with you, partner."

"I'll give you whatever time you want . . . once dinner is served. Now get your ass in gear."

"I'm not starting the pasta until they are here. Did you fire up the heaters yet?"

"Not yet. I have all three Amaretto Sour cheesecakes on ice in the serving coolers, but I gotta say – doesn't seem like a great dessert choice for a party celebrating kids. I have to ask, Scott. Do you think you went a little over-the-top for this one?"

"Nope, got it covered. Emma's famous home-made ice-cream and snickerdoodles are already here. Dessert is covered. Are the bottles of Chianti on the tables?"

"Yep! We're ready, Scott. Stop stressing. Everything is going to be fine."

"When does the puppy get here? And more importantly, where's it going when it does?"

"Emma's son dropped off the crate before heading to the courthouse. I have the extra-large crate hidden behind the photo booth on the lanai. As far as the puppy goes, that's Isaac's problem. Not ours. So, one more time. What's really wrong?"

"I'm getting married in sixty-three days, and I feel like my own reception is taking a back seat to work and getting Amuse Bouche off the ground. Teaching full-time no longer seems practical especially because this school year is slowly killing me. The new social studies curriculum is bad. Really bad. My classroom is a mess and my desk is buried with the million papers the kids have been doing the last two weeks because I have no time to grade anything. I'm cooking until midnight almost every night for the next weekend event. My kitchen sucks. I feel completely overwhelmed – I feel like I'm drowning. And instead of trying to enjoy the ride, all I can think about today is how much I want a family right away. But I wonder if we're rushing just a bit."

"Have you talked to Brandon about all this?"

"No. He's just as busy as I am. He's trying to wrap up three big cases by the start of my summer vacation so we can take a quick honeymoon before all the weddings we have booked. Since we set the date, we've been like two ships passing in the night. But I know we need to have that talk and I also have some decisions to make."

"Listen, I'm your partner in this business, and I want Amuse Bouche to be Tampa's premier party-planning company just like you do. So I understand what you're feeling.

I'm exhausted most nights, too. I never expected our little venture to take off and do so well so fast. But here's why I'm also over-the-moon excited. Our first few parties were only for people we worked with. But now we're getting booked by people who were at those parties. Word is spreading, Scott. Our business plan is rock solid, and I can see the light at the end of the tunnel. I had a long talk with the hubs last weekend. Zach is okay with me giving up the paycheck and diving headfirst into full-time party planning. He wants me happy. In fact, I'm picking up my medical coverage through his plan starting next month, and I have enough in savings to cover my bills for six months. I want you to think about two things. First, I feel like you're trying to grab every brass ring at once. Scott, I know you want it all, but does it have to all arrive on the same day? Sounds like you need to have a long talk with your soon-to-be hubby and see what you guys can work out."

"I knew some downtime with my favorite cousin is what I needed today. How'd you get so smart?"

"Baby, I was born this way. Now get your ass in gear because I'm hearing lots of car doors slamming, and we've got people to feed."

"By the way, where are Brandon and I sitting for this lit-tle adventure today?" I question while pulling the appetizer trays out of the fridge.

"With Emma, Luke, Katie, and Shane. Why?"

"I just want to make sure I have a front row seat and a clear view of Mia's face when Isaac presents the puppy. I ex-pect her reaction to be something we'll talk about for years to come!"

This is the last Myers-Miller family event Sierra and I are catering for the foreseeable future, and I couldn't be happier with how the rest of the day played out. All my worries about space and too many people relaxed the minute we all sat down to dinner.

Emma's reaction to Grace walking through the front door was priceless. Since her daughter arrived Emma has kept her hand either on Grace's shoulder or over her hand. It reminds me of how Sophie held tight to Isaac in the courtroom today. Parents and kids. Kids and parents. Someday that will be me.

No one noticed KJ's thirty minute absence during dessert. I couldn't hold back the laughter when Isaac suddenly vanished the minute KJ quietly slipped back into his seat. I knew what was coming, and couldn't wait for Mia's reaction. Just as I predicted, we will be talking about Mia's reaction for years to come. Juniper, a yellow lab mix, was also adopted by the Miller family today. That puppy is going to pee and chew on everything they own.

CHAPTER SEVEN

Scott

Truly Madly Deeply

"I'D LIKE TO have some input on the reception. Since the entire event is at the Terrail farm, I want life-size Jenga, a scavenger hunt, and your brother to sing at the ceremony. Can you live with that?" I hear Brandon utter as I work to fit all my serving dishes back on the bakers rack.

"Um hmm," I absentmindedly respond. My head is spinning a mile a minute. All of Sierra's advice about prioritizing our wants and wishes makes so much sense. One brass ring at a time. I have so much I want to talk about with Brandon tonight. Should I wait for tomorrow though? It's so late and we both look and feel exhausted. My emotions are all over the place. I need talking points. Brandon can be such a distraction and I'll never be able to verbalize everything I need to say if I'm not prepared. I'll wait until tomorrow morning and take him to breakfast. He'll listen better while munching on pancakes at Bruncheries.

The adoption party was a huge success. I've never seen Mia so calm . . . so settled. Emma's eyes were full of tears through most of the evening. With her arm firmly clamped around Grace's shoulder, I heard Luke mention to KJ he had Lightning tickets for the entire family the next day. All of them: Luke, Emma, Isaac, Mia, Charlie, Abby and the kids are firmly ensconced in the Myers-Miller tribe. Brandon missed the introduction of Juniper, the Miller's new puppy. He left the adoption party early to attend a business dinner downtown. Giant mounds of paper cover every square inch of the sofa and coffee table. He did it again. In order to free up his weekend, the work came home. The parents, all four of them, are in town on Sunday to review several last minute wedding details.

"Umm, Scott? What do you think?"

"Yeah, sounds great," I mumble while trying to locate enough space to store eight crockpots.

"So you're okay with wearing Scottish kilts, and shooting flaming arrows over our guest's heads once we say *I Do?*"

"Whatever you want, honey." At the exact moment I fully comprehend his last comment several cupcake tins, my stack of metal bowls, and one gigantic roll of plastic wrap falls from the third shelf of the bakers rack. "Shit!" I holler while moving out of the way and allowing everything to fall to the tile floor. If the neighbors were sleeping, they aren't anymore. "I need more space! Fuck!" With one easy move I slide my back down the wall and land in a heap on my kitchen floor.

"Hey. Are you okay?" Brandon questions while grasping my hands hoping to help me up. Instead I tug his arm with conviction forcing him to the floor next to me.

"We need to talk. Actually, I need to talk," I whisper with a few tears swimming in my eyes.

"Okay, let's talk. First, answer me. Are you okay? Did you get hurt?"

"I'm fine physically, except for being exceptionally tired. I'm drained emotionally. I want to talk, but I wanted to be more prepared for this chat. You can be very distracting, Brandon Lawrence."

"Scott, are we okay? You're not calling off the wedding – are you?"

"No! Hell no! My God, Brandon! Where did that come from?" I answer with a shocked tone. Shit! We've been working way too much. Weeks ago we promised to never allow work to interfere with our time again and here we are. I guess that conversation is happening tonight after all.

"We're days away from getting married, and you're getting all serious on me while looking like you want to cry. I know we haven't been spending a lot of time together. I've been worried because there are days I feel you slipping away from me. Wow, Scott, you just scared the shit out of me!" Brandon's arms rest behind his neck somewhat blocking his beautiful face. When I tug his hands into mine, it's hard to keep from kissing him senseless. Stay focused. We need to talk.

"I love you, moron! I love your body, your mind, and your soul. But I need you to listen to everything I have to say before you start problem solving. I know you, Brandon Lawrence. As soon as I mention something is bothering me, you'll forget the need to talk and just start fixing things. There is no crisis, okay?"

With his sweet school-boy smile and a chaste kiss, my man settles back to listen. Get this right. Go slow. Simply state facts.

"Okay. Tell me what's on your mind." We both settle back against the kitchen wall, but I refuse to let go of his hand. This is Brandon. My Brandon. He steadies me. He loves me like no one else can.

"I'm not loving teaching anymore. I want to take a leave of absence at the end of this school year and focus on the business full-time."

"Okay. That's doable," he answers calmly.

With shock etched in my expression I can't believe what he just said. "Like really doable?"

"We might have to slash the wedding budget a bit, but yeah . . . doable."

"I need a bigger kitchen."

"I know."

"And as much as I want kids, I think we need to wait. We need a house first."

"I agree completely."

"As soon as we're married, you'll need to pick up my medical coverage."

"Piece of cake."

"Will you please take care of that this week?"

"Not a problem. I can fill out the initial paperwork on-line this weekend."

"And we're not wearing kilts and shooting flaming arrows at our guests."

"Ah, so you were listening."

"Yes, I was. That was so much easier than I thought it would be. I love you so much."

"I love you, too. Can I talk now? I have a few ideas."

"Absolutely. Solve all my problems. Please."

"First, as far as I know you and Sierra don't have any functions between now and our wedding. Still correct?"

"No. We have one small function for Sierra's boss mid-March. But it's during my spring break. Why?"

"Promise me . . . nothing else before our wedding. You're exhausted and I want our wedding to be fabulous. Concentrate on our party. Agreed?"

"Agreed. I'll let Sierra know."

"If my sister helps you, can you handle the centerpieces yourself? The flowers are a big line item in the wedding budget."

"I'll ask Sierra to hook me up with her flower guy. I'm sure I can pick up what we need wholesale and that should save at least half of the flower budget."

"What about the cake? I'd rather have whatever you'd make anyway. If you stick to your promise and don't book any other functions, will you have time to design our wedding cake?"

"Yes. I can go with cupcakes. Storage is the main issue."

"I have a solution for that as well. More on that later. Now the honeymoon. Instead of the week-long New York trip, what about four days in Sin City instead? Mariah Carey is playing Vegas now and hotel rooms are cheap in July. And for the record, I was kidding about life-size Jenga. If we make these and a few more small changes, we'll still have the wedding of our dreams and can save about $5,000. Talk to your principal this week, Scott. I want you happy and I see how much you dig working with Sierra. If your heart's not in teaching anymore, take a step back next year. We will make it work."

"I want to grow my business, but how are we ever going to afford our dream home if I'm not working?"

"Things are picking up for me at work. My dinner meeting tonight was very successful. I signed CS Indie Publishing tonight. They've had a banner year and they need my expert negotiating skills for a few upcoming projects. One of their authors just got tapped by Lionsgate Production. They want to option one of her books – maybe even the entire series. I expect my end-of-the-year pay-out to be substantial. And, I also expect Amuse Bouche to have a banner first year. We'll be okay, Scott. I want to start looking at houses this summer."

"Well then, if I'm diving head-first into full-time catering and party planning this kitchen doesn't work. I don't have enough counter space or storage," I mutter while stacking the metal bowls.

"Remember I said I had an idea? You know Mrs. Horvath who lives across the hall?"

"Yeah, I love Helen. What's up?"

"She's a new grandmother. Her daughter just gave birth to triplets last week. She's heading to Denver for an extended stay to help the family – at least through August. She asked if we could take care of her cats and water the plants. When I told her all about your business and how much you needed either a bigger or second kitchen she offered her place while she's gone in exchange. Of course, I said I'd check with you first. What do you think?"

"I think you're a genius. Helen did a remodel about two years ago. Her kitchen is twice the size as ours. We'll need to offer her some sort of financial compensation, though. Maybe pay her electric bill? The business can afford that. I'll be using all her appliances and will have to keep the air conditioning running full blast all summer while cooking. I think that's a fair trade. What do you think?"

When Brandon ponders something serious the corners of his eyes pull together tightly and he closes out the world by drawing the shades to his soul. His eyelids gently close as he turns his head slightly right while chewing on his left thumbnail. He obviously has been giving this entire scenario a lot of thought, almost as if he's been preparing for my mini-breakdown tonight. "I'd like to draw up some sort of rental agreement between Amuse Bouche and Helen. That way whatever you pay can be applied to your business expenditures and therefore is a tax write-off."

"Did I mention how much I love you? And how much you right my world every day? I feel like a hundred pound weight has been lifted from my shoulders." For a brief moment I stop to run my thumb along his bottom lip and think about taking him right here and right now. But we did just decide without much conversation to hold off on adopting until we find a house, and that could take some time. Part of me wonders if that's what he really wants. "Are you sure you're okay pushing pause on adopting right now? Sometimes I wonder if every decision you make is just to give me what I want. What do you want, Brandon? I'm so sorry, honey. I never asked you that."

Scott, you should know by now I'm happy when you're happy. I want kids with you. After today, going through the entire adoption process with Isaac and Mia – I know I want to be a parent. And someday, we'll make terrific dads. Everything we just decided puts us on that path to those babies that will someday be ours. You're right, we need a house. Besides, since we said we'd adopt siblings, and work within the foster care system, we could end up with as many as four kids all at once. And when that time comes, I want you to be able to stay home with our family for a few years. Getting Amuse Bouche up and running before kids makes sense."

Sliding up to my knees, I pull Brandon's lips to mine in one urgent and frenzied kiss. I lift my free hand and run my palm down the length of his left thigh and back up the right side leaving it to rest at the juncture of where right meets left. Pulling back slightly with my mouth still covering his I manage to squeak out one simple statement and question, "You smell good. Did you already have a shower?"

Leaning in, the tip of his nose brushes against the pulse

point of my throat as he takes one deep breath. "I did. But I could use another," he whispers once his tongue finds the outer shell of my ear. "I'd like to fuck you in the shower. Now."

Before I have a chance to utter 'hell yes' his arms come around me, tugging at my hair, and lifting my eager lips to his. My body hardens with expectation and hunger as our tongues intertwine once again. Roughly he guides me out of the kitchen, pulling urgently at my belt, my tie and my shirt. I want to lose myself in him, or better yet lose myself to him tonight. "I'm all yours, babe. You take me any way you want tonight," I practically yell while toeing off my shoes and socks.

The bathroom fills with steam quickly. Brandon stalks me backward toward the tiled wall with such force the towel rack breaks its connection with the wall and falls to the floor. His grip on my face and my hair is almost painful as he suckles my lower lip, nipping and biting as his tongue invades my mouth furiously. Using one leg, he parts mine forcefully and begins his sensual assault. His tongue travels the length of my body tormenting my nipples, my naval, and eventually the tip of my rock hard erection. I practically growl as a result and push my pelvis toward his awaiting mouth. And then I'm there. Completely seated, watching every move his mouth now makes. Brandon has no gag reflex . . . at all. He sucks hard running his tongue up and down and in and out of his mouth, finally to the back of the throat. I love watching him bring me to my knees.

Nearly humming with anticipation, I am so close. If his

tongue moves any faster over the head of my penis I'll explode upon impact. And that's when he gently pulls away massaging the sweet spot right under the thin skin with his thumb and forefinger. "Did you like that, babe?" Before I can answer his finger slides up my back side and very gently begins to work the opening. "I want to fuck you, Scott. It's been weeks since I've been inside you. Do you want toys to start or just me?"

Feeling the penetration of a finger and then a second, I gasp welcoming the intrusion. "Just you. Only you tonight." The shower has been running for at least fifteen minutes and the steam from the heated water fills the air and coats my body in moisture. Carefully, Brandon's hands and body guide us into the walk-in shower. Our gigantic shower is what sold me on the condo during our very first visit. With four shower heads, water rains from all directions. Brandon's body covers my back side against the shower wall pinning my hands overhead. Settling my right knee on the shower seat, I'm anxious to have him inside me. I crave his proximity, his intrusion into my body, as his mouth and teeth settle into the back of my neck.

"Keep your hands pressed into the wall, babe," Brandon warns as he grips my cock with one hand while penetrating my opening with a slow and careful pace. Once firmly seated inside, he begins to work my rock hard erection with the friction of his hand. His teeth continue to graze my neck and shoulders. That sensation causes me to scream an unintelligible phrase of delight. When he begins to move his body at the same rhythm as his hand I know I won't last long. "Fuck,

Scott. So tight. So close. Stay with me." His hand picks up a faster pace, and I know neither one of us will last much longer. Brandon can't stop talking and his whispered words are charging my release. "God! You feel so good. Together, babe. With me, Scott."

"Almost, Oh God!" I can barely hold it together as Brandon grips my length tighter and pumps both his hand and body at a slightly faster clip. We don't fuck often enough and I almost stop breathing as his motions bring me to the brink. I lose my breath sucking in sharply as I feel him hardening inside of me. The intrusion, although foreign, is so welcome.

"I love you, Scott. I'm ready. Let go with me, babe," he whispers in my ear as I turn my head to find his mouth. I feel his legs stiffen and feel whimpers pour into my mouth as he detonates inside of me and I explode in his hand. Our bodies shake with aftershocks for several minutes as we sink to the shower floor. "Okay, babe?" Brandon asks while beginning his second sensual assault, washing and massaging me from head to toe. I'm one big pile of sated man, finding it impossible to lift my arms or keep my eyes open. "Scott? Did I hurt you?"

"No, honey, quite the opposite. I'm just a pile of skin and bones. After that, I'll definitely sleep tonight. And you could never hurt me, Brandon. You know my body all too well. When and where to push the limits, and exactly the moment to dial everything back. If you can top that orgasm on our honeymoon, I'll give you a million dollars."

"A million bucks, huh? We'll need to practice a lot before Vegas then," he whispers while laughing lightly.

We sit in comfortable silence as the soft cloth covered in my favorite body wash skims over my skin. My shoulders are treated to deeper pressure as my neck cracks twice. Turning to the love of my life, I offer him a kiss that says what I can't verbalize at this moment. I quite literally have no will to move. "I just want to sleep for about fourteen hours," I mumble against Brandon's chest.

"Do you have plans tomorrow?" He asks while helping me to stand and shutting down the shower.

"I brought home a ton of papers to grade. I seriously hate grading papers. I'm pretty sure everyone's getting an 'A or B' this week. I'm sleeping until noon, and then I'm taking my soon-to-be hubby to dinner."

"Any place special?"

"Doesn't matter. Every dinner is special when I sit across from you."

CHAPTER EIGHT

Scott

What a Wonderful World

"WHICH DRESS TO you prefer, darling?" My mother questions while presenting three selections. To be honest, they all look the same. They're all blue. They're all cocktail length and the necklines are identical. It honestly doesn't matter but she'll never make a choice without my stamp of approval. Brandon's mother is so much easier to work with. I showed her a dress made of the most beautiful light green fabric that I thought was perfect for her slender frame. She bought it the next day, and we moved onto and purchased shoes 24 hours later.

"I like the second one, mom. It's the perfect shade of blue for your coloring, and I love the pleated skirt. I can't

53

wait to watch you float around the dance floor in that dress," I answer with as much enthusiasm as I can muster.

"What about me, son? Traditional suit or tuxedo?"

"Dad, I think a traditional blue suit would be perfect. I'd really like it if you would wear a bow tie similar to mine. Anthony already agreed to a dark green necktie."

Since Brandon and I are saying *I Do* outdoors, we're keeping our wardrobe clean and simple, combining shades of blues and greens in all the fabrics with white flowers everywhere to brighten the darker shades. I'm wearing a dark blue bow tie, the closest I could find to mirror the color of my eyes. Brandon will be sporting a darker, kelly green necktie. When I look into Brandon's eyes, it's like swimming in chocolate. But occasionally, when the light falls just right, dark pools of gold streak from his pupils. The dark green will draw out the gold. Other than that, we're keeping the wardrobe modest. Dark tan slacks, matching lighter tan dress shirts, our ties, Brandon in a tweed jacket with kelly green elbow pads, and me in the somewhat matching vest with dark blue accents at the pockets and along the trim. Everything designed by Ted Baker or Hugo Boss – it is our wedding ensemble after all.

My brother, Anthony, will be standing next to me with Brandon's brother, Jimmy next to him. To be honest, I was surprised Brandon didn't ask his sister Evie to stand next to him. He and Evie are exceptionally close. We rarely spend time with Jimmy and his wife, choosing to hang with his sister every chance we have. Lately we've been meeting with the charming couple for breakfast nearly every Sunday morning. Evie continues to be my saving grace with wedding plans, stepping up to help whenever and with whatever she can. At eight months pregnant, she believes her appearance might take the limelight away from her big brother and me. She wants this day to be only about us. It was her idea to stay in the background on this momentous occasion by presenting several ceremony readings and organizing wardrobes. Now Brandon has drafted her to help me with table centerpieces along with all the corsages and boutonnieres.

"I have one more surprise, darling," my mother announces with glee. "Anthony has heard from all the boys of ACTS and they've accepted our invitation for your big day. Anthony needs to know if you've made your musical selections for the ceremony, or if they have carte blanche to perform something of their choice."

"Mom, you invited all the guys? What? They all said yes?" I ask with trepidation. The last time I saw Chris he had that girl he suddenly worshipped sitting on his lap at the barbeque my parents hosted for my high school graduation. I haven't seen him in over ten years and wonder if he came out to his family. I wonder if anyone has ever considered the two of us an item since we were inseparable our senior year. Crap!

"Of course, sweet boy! I knew you'd be surprised."

"Surprised isn't the word I'd use, Mama. Their names were never on any guest list. Mom, we're already pushing the limits for this venue. We can't go over 250 guests."

"I know. But Anthony was so excited when he finally heard from Aiden and that snowballed out of my control within minutes. Anthony and Aiden found Connor and Sean within twenty-four hours, and suddenly it was only a matter of finding the last two guys. This seems right, Scott. You boys had a brotherhood that was something pretty impressive."

Brandon is watching me closely and given how well he reads every one of my moods, he knows I'm silently falling apart. I never wanted the guys to sing. Just my brother with maybe Aiden on guitar. It's been over a decade since I've seen or talked to Sean, Tyler, Connor or Chris. How can I negotiate this? "Mom, I really just want Anthony to sing."

"Don't be ridiculous, Scott. It's all settled. The boys really want to do this for you, and so many folks from back home just can't wait to hear the boys of ACTS again. Now, can we talk menu items?"

"The menu is done, Mama. I signed the contract with the caterer last week. My order is placed with the wholesale florist Sierra uses. The vases have been ordered and should be here the first week of March. We have the invitations ready to mail and we put the final touches on wardrobe today. Our DJ has been hired, I pick up Brandon's ring next week, and the menu is set in stone. The flower girl dresses have been shipped and I expect them any day now. I haven't picked my flavors of cupcakes yet, but I know I want a selection of five. My best girls from work are going to serve cake the day of – so they'll help me decide what to bake," I answer attempting to move the discussion away from anything wedding. Normally I love talking about all my plans, but with my mother's revelation that the boys of ACTS are making an appearance, I suddenly feel bewildered.

"Son, why aren't you using one or two of your little cousins as flower girls? I mean, your flower girls aren't even family," my mother questions with indignation.

Before I can say a word, Brandon's courtroom voice suddenly booms over the table. "Marjorie, Mia Miller is one of Scott's closet friends. They're like brother and sister, so it makes sense to have her daughters in the wedding. Here, in Tampa, the Myers-Miller clan has become our family of sorts. Scott wants them part of our ceremony, and quite frankly so do I. We're not having children that belong to some random cousin as part of our wedding party. The people we choose to stand with us are exactly that. Our choice."

For the first time in my mother's life she has no comeback. Rising from her chair she finds her way to the kitchen and teapot full of her favorite lavender tea. Silence is golden, unless you have a mother like mine. Then silence is suspicious – very, very suspicious.

I was so looking forward to having all the parents here today, but my mother's attempt to add a layer of Mississippi snob appeal to our wedding is about to push me over the edge, and I won't have it. "Here's what you can do, dad. There are three hotels within five minutes of the venue. I have blocks of rooms set aside at each location. Let's get a flyer together and out to family so they get their rooms booked now before they're all gone. And then let's get to lunch. I'm famished," I plead with a forced smile. This family gathering can't end soon enough, and I can see the gears shifting in Brandon's head. He's curious about my firm desire to shut down the ACTS performance at our wedding. To be honest, I'm curious as well. Why do I suddenly care? I should be thanking Chris for setting me on my path to Brandon Lawrence.

"Honey, I really think you should allow your cousin, Sierra, to be a guest at your wedding. Why are you insisting she stay on as your wedding coordinator, sweetheart? You know I'd be happy to take over," my mama confesses while straightening her skirt.

The day . . . this VERY LONG day is finally winding down as I lift my parents' bags from the trunk of Brandon's car. The airport drop-off zone is crazy, and the airport cop keeps blowing his whistle in our direction. "Mama, I love you, but this is what Sierra does. And I might add, she does it to perfection. That way you can enjoy the day without worry. Believe me Amuse Bouche has it all under control and our work with Alfonso's Catering has gone really well." I don't know how to spell it out any clearer. We have the best of all worlds. We have Sierra, and she is the Queen of Party Planning, and Adam at Alfonso's has been a dream to work with. This is the start of an excellent partnership which I'm sure will fuel lots of new business.

"If you say so, darling. I'll have Anthony give you a call to go over the music. I think you should consider having your first dance to something the boys sing?"

Shut this down right away. "Brandon and I already picked our song. Why don't you pick something for the mother/son dance? I give you free reign to pick anything you want. Now get moving before I get a ticket and you all miss your plane. I love you both so much." With that my parents hustle into the terminal and away from my wondering glance.

"That wasn't so bad," Brandon howls as I climb into the passenger seat and we move off the airport grounds. "Your mama feels left out, my love. Give her something to do, please. Otherwise, she's going to start poking her nose into all our wedding plans and you know that spells disaster. Now, why'd you freak out over the boys singing?"

"I didn't freak out!"

"Yes Scott, yes you did. What's going on?"

"The boys weren't on the guest list, Brandon. Everybody at work is coming AND bringing their plus one. I know all the stats. Twenty percent of invitees will decline the invite. But we're the first gay wedding for our crowd. Believe me, everybody is showing up. We're going to be way over 250 and that, my soon-to-be husband, is a problem."

"I agree that's an issue. When we're home let's look at the guest list again and see where we can trim a little fat!" He blurts out with laughter. "And then when you're ready, tell me the real reason you freaked."

"Brandon, Chris was my first. Like my real honest-to-God first gay experience. No one back home knows that. We kept the whole thing on the down-low the entire time. I'm not even sure Chris ever came out, or if he's still in hiding and pretending to be somebody he's not. I haven't seen him in ten years. We never said goodbye. We were never official- ly anything. We played almost every weekend during our junior and senior years but never had a single conversation about what was happening to us."

"So maybe it's a good thing he's showing up? Maybe you both need a little closure?"

"I don't think you get it. IF he's out, and I'm out, then the entire town is going to put it all together and the rest of the guys will feel – "

"Feel what? And more importantly, who cares? We're talking history, Scott. This happened many years ago, and people will just have to deal with it."

"Brandon, we're talking about people who still fly a Confederate flag, and in the confines of their own home believe I'm – we're an abomination. My extended family is showing up for our ceremony ONLY because curiosity killed the cat. Chris' dad was a deacon – probably still is a deacon in our church. This has the potential to start some fireworks and I don't want that anywhere near our wedding. That's why I'm worried."

"Let's get the boys of ACTS here a few days early for re- hearsal. That way you and Chris will have some time to clear the air before the ceremony. If we know there's a potential disaster brewing, we need to be proactive. Call your brother once we're home. I think it's time I meet Mr. First."

CHAPTER NINE

Scott

I Won't Give Up

"OKAY, SCOTT, WE'VE prepared a little fun tonight," Mia announces with a light in her eyes. "This is your final fling before the ring! So we are taking you on a scavenger hunt tonight, my friend! Be prepared for numerous shots, tons of silliness, and a few embarrassing moments." My best girls have prepped a little party for me to celebrate my now legal right to marry Mr. Brandon Lawrence. I cannot believe it's actually happening! In thirteen days, I become Scott Wilson-Lawrence.

"I'll handle the first item on the list!" Emma shouts. While skimming over the entire paper Emma's eye's dance with laughter. Finally she shakes her head and wears one beautiful smile. Whatever she chose must be something pretty tame.

"First, does everyone have a drink?" Julia hollers while working the bar. Within minutes she's placed a small shot-glass in everyone's hand. No surprise here. Sex on the beach.

When Emma begins, her eyes light with love as she raises her glass. "It's my honor to give tonight's first toast. Our very dear friend, Scott, will finally say *I Do* in just thir-teen short days. Our message for you, my friend, is clear. Be happy. Be in love every day by reminding yourself each morning the reasons you chose to say *I Do*. Remember even though you're married, you still need to date. Keep a list of places and activities he mentions he'd love to see or do, and then surprise him on some random Saturday when no plans have been made. Have a picnic on the floor when rain inter-rupts a special date you've planned. Hang out at Starbucks and read a book together while holding hands. Watch the sunrise and sunset in the same day. Be creative with the time you have together."

Mia suddenly rises and with fresh tears swimming in those beautiful green eyes, she continues, "Kiss every morn-ing, kiss every time one of you has to leave and then also upon return. Be sure to kiss every night before you say good-night. Kiss him every day like your life depends on it. Because it does."

"Make sure you put the toilet seat down after you pee," Julia chuckles and then brings her toast to a halt. "Wait, maybe that one doesn't really matter in your case. Okay. Brandon is hot and sexy and he loves you, pal. Tell him ev-ery day how lucky you are that he chose you to be his family." With her smile now lost Julia's eyes are diverted from our party for a brief moment, mumbling into thin air. Her mood has improved somewhat during the last few weeks, but she's distancing herself from our crowd and retreating inward more and more. Emma and I share a quick glance that Mia acknowledges with concern. Tomorrow, the three of us need to talk.

Rebecca is our resident crier and I wonder if she'll be able to get through her entire toast. "I know you spend a lot of time in the kitchen as cooking is your business. But your man's eyes light up like nothing I've seen before when he tastes one of your heavenly creations. Scott, remember to fill Brandon's belly with his favorite meals often. Eat together at your table each and every night, even when it's take-out. Use your nice dishes now and then to remind your man he's worth the time it took to pull out the good china."

"Never let anything fester. If you're angry, be angry – and talk about the reasons you feel the way you feel," Katie whispers while reaching for Emma's hand. "When you argue, and yes you will argue – fight fair. Words are powerful, my friend. Beautiful words heal and protect, and give you a hundred reasons why your marriage is worth fighting for. Ugly words cut, leave scars, and wound the heart."

Evie, Brandon's sister, rises from her seat with her eyes brimming, and raises her club soda. I'm beginning to wonder if this party with my best girls is heading toward a major cryfest. "Don't become a neat freak, Scott. That's my best advice. Brandon's middle name should be neat freak. Help him find the comfort in comfortable. Live in your house – that's what makes your house your home. But I would also like to add, please put the toilet seat down after you pee. Because it does really matter. Remember, whether you guys have little boys or little girls someday – they need to learn that!"

"And remember my dear cousin, Brandon is hot. Like freakishly beautiful. You need to tap the boy any time there's an opportunity. Have sex all the time. I want you experiencing jaw-dropping, panty twisting, hot-as-hell sex every day for as long as your body can take it!" Sierra challenges as the rest of the girls attempt to hold back giggles.

"Sierra! Geeze that's my brother you're talking about. I'll never get that picture out of my head now." I agree, Evie – not an image I want my best girls to have.

"To Scott and Brandon!" Emma hollers while tipping back her shot with ease. The rest of the ladies follow suit with screams of well wishes and blessings. "Julia, why don't you get Scott started on the rest of his hunt. I think you should take care of the second item on the list yourself." Smiles and giggles wash over everyone's faces and I now know I'm in for quite a night.

"No problem. I've got this. Who has the Sharpies?" Rebecca digs out red and black Sharpies from her purse and passes both markers along to Julia. "Let's hit the crapper, Mr. Bachelor. I'm giving you an ass tattoo that you won't be able see or wash off for at least a week! Brandon's gonna thank me for this in the morning."

Before the night is over my best girls have managed to take my picture with two beat cops, coax me onto the stage to sing with the cover band, talk me into kissing a bald man's head, drink a blow job shot from between some random guy's legs, and pass out condoms to everyone in the bar. I'm sure there is more, but by midnight my head is spinning as this is the most I've had to drink in one night in years. I know it may seem weird or strange, but I feel as though I'm crossing some arbitrary line tonight. From single and carefree to responsible and taken. Even though Brandon and I have been together for three years and living together for the past year I know I've just taken my first step down the aisle.

By 2:00 a.m. I'm surround by my best girls in a circular booth at the Village Inn. After inhaling two stacks of blueberry pancakes and about a pound of hickory smoked bacon, I can't handle another bite. The girls kept me hydrated tonight, and as the effects of the alcohol begin to wear off I'm surprised there's no evidence of a hangover. The ladies' chatter is vulgar, their giggling is deafening, and I couldn't be happier.

"Scott, how did you and Brandon meet? Either I missed that story or you've never shared," Rebecca questions as the table chatter falls into silence.

"Yeah! I don't think either one of you have ever shared that story," Evie announces to our group.

"It's not a very exciting story," I lie. "The details are actually quite boring."

"Let us be the judge!" Katie shrieks. "I can't believe how much fun I had tonight. I love being a mom and cuddling with Lucy every day, but I really needed out tonight! All right, Scott! Out with it – your stories are the highlight of my monotonous life."

"I think you all are going to be very disappointed." I stop for a brief moment to recall the first time I saw my man and almost lost him before I had him. My expression must give way to a silly smile and Julia can barely contain herself.

"Oh ladies, I think our friend here has a great story to tell! You did it in a bar bathroom or his car, right?" Julia squeals while clapping her hands.

"Not that exciting, Julia. Sorry to disappoint. I saw Brandon at my local grocery store early one Friday evening. When I first saw him, I noticed his cart was overloaded, picking up what looked like several weeks' worth of groceries. I admired the view and then moved through the store focused on my mission. I was supposed to be slipping in and grabbing mixers for a party with a few friends on Causeway Beach. I saw Brandon up close and personal while he was studying a bottle of wine. I was mesmerized. I can still picture it. It was late October, and there was a bit of a chill in the air. He was sporting a grey Hugo Boss suit. Remember, it's early evening, and after a full day the man still looked impeccable as well as edible. His clothes were all designer wear, down to the dark violet tie and the Cole Hann shoes. Shoes are the telltale sign, ladies. They weren't new but they were recently buffed and polished. His hair was cut to perfection, but just like now, his morning scruff had grown throughout the day and shadowed his face perfectly. I stopped dead in my tracks barely able to breathe or keep my eyes off him."

"So, did he notice you staring? Did you use some cheesy pick-up line?" Mia asks with such a sweet smile.

"Actually . . . no. We exchanged a smile or two and then I picked up my mixers and went to my party."

Emma shakes her head almost understanding my slow approach. "I'm not surprised. So, how did you finally meet?"

"The moment I left the store, I felt flustered. I almost went back in and introduced myself, but I was also anxious to party. But I should have gone back. For weeks, I thought about him every night when I went to bed and dreamt about him all night long. I was so pissed at myself for walking away that night. For the next four Friday nights, I went grocery shopping at the same time hoping to run in to him again. I bought so much food I had to invite each one of you to dinner multiple times over the next several weeks. I played around with a few new recipes and brought a ton of food to work every day. Remember?" Several of my best girls nod, while Julia seems completely transfixed by my story. "My mission became wandering those aisles week after week. On the fourth week I was ready to give up. I was certain I'd never see him again. Feeling a bit lost and sorry for myself, I headed to the wine aisle, picking up and studying the same bottle of wine he had in his hands four weeks earlier. When I turned to leave – there he stood. All I could think to say to him was 'It's about time.' He smiled, I introduced myself, got his number, and asked him to a late Sunday lunch. The rest as they say, is history." Turning to avoid everyone's heated gaze, my blushing is difficult to disguise.

"There's more to that story. I'd bet a week's pay," Julia announces to the crowd.

"Nope. That's it. You asked how we met. That's how we

met."

"But there's more that happened that night. Right? Tell us all about the first time you had sex!" Julia asks through a huge smile.

"That would be a definite NO! First off, Evie is here. And for the record, I never kiss and tell."

"I think your story is beautiful, Scott. It's also nearly three in the morning, ladies. I think it's time to get Mr. Bachelor home," Emma mentions while signing the receipt. "Who's riding with me?" My girl knows how to shut Julia down, and for that, I'm incredibly grateful. The memories of our first meeting leave me with a silly smile and a little pep in my step. I certainly enjoyed that walk down memory lane.

Once home I tip-toe around our bedroom while Brandon sleeps soundly, breathing slow and deep. After finishing in the bathroom I notice our perfect, neat and tidy bedroom and remember Evie's toast. Before climbing in next to the love of my life, I lay his robe across the side chair and place his slippers near the foot of the bed. Once snuggled in next to my love, Brandon's breathing is hypnotic, guiding me to relax as I recall the rest of our story.

"Oh my God!" I mutter under my breath. "It's about time."

His lips give way to an infectious school-boy smile as he extends his hand. "Hello. I'm Brandon. Brandon Lawrence." Hmmm, well dressed – Hugo Boss suit and Cole Hann shoes. The man knows how to pull it all altogether. I'm pretty sure the violet tie is Hugo Boss, too. God! Wish I wasn't sporting Pride Middle School spirit shirt.

"Hi. Scott Wilson," I enunciate clearly. *His hand is soft, and well kept. Recent manicure. Oh . . . and very big. His grasp practically smothers my small hand.*

"Nice to finally meet you, Scott," he says with twinkling eyes. *What a smile!*

"You, too." *His gaze nearly brings me to my knees. Those have to be the darkest brown eyes I've ever seen. They're the color of milk chocolate. Edible.* "Finally?"

"Honestly? I wanted to talk to you four weeks ago. I thought you were interested, too. But you moved around the store so fast and left so abruptly, I decided you probably weren't interested at all." *His solemn tone and falling smile says a lot. I like that he's taller than me.*

"I was. Still am. I am most definitely interested," I answer in an authoritative tone. "I've been shopping here every Friday night at eight for the last four weeks hoping to run into you again."

"I bought ten bottles of this Sauvignon Blanc, four boxes of cereal and twelve pounds of chicken chasing you around this store four weeks ago. I didn't know what to do with it all. I don't even cook."

"You did?" I ask as we begin a staring contest. *Who will blink first?*

"I did."

"I can cook." *Food. Always my savior. Bet this opens the door.*

"You do?"

"It's late. Did you have dinner yet?" I ask boldly.

"No. You?"

"No. What else did you pick up following me around the grocery that night?"

"I know I have frozen vegetables and microwavable macaroni and cheese in the freezer."

"Ugh! I guess that will have to do. Someday I'll make you my signature macaroni and cheese dish. You'll never eat that frozen shit again. Do you have sugar, flour, spices, soy sauce?"

Damn! He's so hot and he looks kind of cute when he's confused. "Umm . . . not sure. Remember, I don't cook."

"Walk with me. I'll pick up what we need. And then, Mr. Brandon Lawrence, I'm making you dinner. There will be leftovers – I want you thinking about me all week."

Some stories need a little privacy and there's no reason to share details. No one needs to know I followed Brandon to his condo that night and didn't leave until Sunday. No one needs to know on Sunday, I took him for that late lunch, and then made him dinner again that night. No one needs to know I didn't go home for an entire week.

With a smile beaming from ear to ear I turn my body toward Brandon and gently tug him into my side. My chin rests over top his head while my fingers lightly caress his cheek. I knew the first time I saw him. I knew he would love any meal I created for him with his twelve pounds of chicken. I knew I was home the minute I walked into this condo. I knew I loved him the moment he offered me his hand and said his name. The rest as they say, is history.

CHAPTER TEN

Scott

Thinking Out Loud

"ANTHONY!" GOD! I miss my big brother so much.
"Little brother – Scott! It's so good to see you, man. It's been too long." I feel my brother's arms wrap around me and hang on for dear life. He's always been my best friend, but for the last eight years our homes have fallen in two different states, and we do not see each other nearly enough. For a brief moment I question his choice to stay in our hometown and wonder if my big brother will ever find the happiness he truly deserves.

"Way too long." I practically whisper while pulling him in for one more hug. Brandon makes the tight turn from his home office into our great room with a welcoming smile warming my heart. He won my brother over at their very first meet and greet.

"Anthony!" Brandon bellows while enveloping my brother, all six feet seven inches of him, in a tight hug. "Welcome. We've missed you, friend. So where's the rest of your rat pack gang? I've been hearing about the boys of ACTS for several years, I've seen pictures, but this weekend will be my first opportunity to actually hear your music."

"It's good to see you, too, Brandon. Aiden and his wife, Franny, are checking into the hotel as we speak. I think Franny is about six months along. They're expecting a baby boy sometime in July. The trip wore her out and she mentioned something about swollen feet and a nap. The rest of the guys are rolling in over the next several hours."

"Everybody gets in tonight?" I manage to squeak out.

"Yeah, and we thought since all the wedding stuff shifts into high gear tomorrow we'd take the two of you out tonight. I made reservations at Ocean Prime. You guys want to avoid Mom and Dad this evening?" Anthony offers with a mischievous twinkle in his eyes.

"Hell yes," both Brandon and I blurt out at once.

"Good. Mind if I hang here and we ride together? I'd rather not sit in an empty hotel room all afternoon. Mom would probably find me and –"

"Absolutely. Stay. But know that I'm working on some wedding stuff right now. Brandon's sister, Evie, and a work friend are helping me build the centerpieces today. Let's catch up over flowers for a few hours."

The rest of the afternoon is spent over at our wedding command center, AKA, our neighbor, Helen's condo. I proudly update my big brother on my decision to step away from teaching to concentrate on the business full-time. His happiness for my decision is genuine and his encouraging words are welcome. Here's hoping the parents handle the news just as well. Evie and Julia welcome Anthony as only they could do. Put him to work. Julia's no-nonsense approach to almost everything seems to pique Anthony's interest in flower arranging. Evie's sweet and good-natured personality coupled with Julia's sarcastic tone and Anthony's quick wit make for an interesting afternoon. My brother is good people. I wish he'd move to Tampa so he can hang with us more often.

Sierra loaded up Helen's family room with several banquet tables that we pushed together to make one giant workspace. Over the last three months the tables have been covered with everything from address lists, stamps, photos, invitations, to white linen napkins that I folded and ironed to look like a man's necktie, to the twenty-five large cylindrical vases now awaiting flowers. Over the course of the next two hours we manage to attach the ribbon and bow to each vase and separate some of the initial greenery into each container as well. The rest of the flowers arrive tomorrow afternoon.

I watch my brother through a comfortable gaze and wonder if he's happy. Anthony and I have always been exceptionally close. He had my back as a kid, allowing no one to take advantage of my good nature. But we were always very different. Anthony was our family athlete, a big burly football player, and secured a full ride to Mississippi State after graduation. But he struggled in the world of academia needing a constant tutor. When he dropped out of school and moved home I had no idea what to say or do to help him. The fact of the matter is, Anthony was and still is far more musically talented than me. I wonder why he never pursued a music education and career. For now, he seems rock solid, but I worry about him a lot. He still lives in our hometown and works for our father. And if I know our mother, he's been set up on more blind dates that he'd care to admit.

I, on the other hand, loved sports – from afar. I was the family genius, or so my mother thought. Was I a genius? Probably not. Instead, I was creative as hell. I worked and studied like a maniac. Every. Single. Day. I wanted out of the little Mississippi town I grew up in, and I needed a scholarship to make it happen. My love and gift for music provided a fabulous financial opportunity, but I never wanted a music career. In fact, music was simply a means to the end. Moving to Tampa at eighteen was an education all in itself. Folks from Tampa will tell you this isn't a big city. But to me, Tampa offered everything I needed. The minute I stepped onto the University of South Florida campus I knew I was home. As a result, I studied like a madman, worked two jobs, and came out to my roommate my freshman year. With ease I managed to hang onto a 3.95 grade point average and graduate with a double major in both music and social science education.

The two of us are alike in some ways but really so very different. I'm thrilled to have some time alone with Anthony to find out if he's really satisfied with his life. I'd love to have him here with me, and think maybe Sierra and I could use a little help with all the summer weddings. What a great idea! Maybe I can slowly pull him out of our hometown and here to Tampa with me.

The afternoon is not a waste. The vases are ready for flowers. Tomorrow Evie and Julia will take care of the arrangements and I will busy myself in the kitchen completing the cakes for the reception. Before I know it, the afternoon has spilled into dusk. I'm dressed in my favorite Ted Baker black suit and on my way to dinner with all the boys of ACTS. Ready or not – time to see Chris.

Brandon and I have never dined at Ocean Prime before and I'm beginning to question why. This restaurant is right up our alley, and the ambiance is completely in line with our style. There's a few side private rooms and it appears Anthony has booked one to give our party some privacy. Aiden and Franny are the first to arrive. Aiden is quite the domineering, over-protective husband – not a role I ever expected him to take on. He was the only guy in ACTS that looked like he didn't belong most of the time. Church wasn't his thing. Anthony was the only reason he continued to show up each Sunday. That and because he just loved to play his guitar. He loved that guitar. With long, unkempt hair and a pair of yellow-tinted sunglasses always perched on his nose, he looked more the rock and roller over church choir boy the entire time we sang together. Now, he looks quite grown-up and very much the high powered corporate executive. But he assures us, he's never put down his guitar.

According to Franny he can hear a tune once and play the entire selection without error five minutes later.

The comfort level so far seems doable and I finally agree with Brandon, that maybe seeing Chris after all these years isn't a bad idea. With the exception of the man of the hour, the rest of the gang pours in. Our time together feels so natural, I'm actually glad my mother insisted the boys of ACTS sing at the wedding. Sean never made it to American Idol, but did make his way into television production. Now gainfully employed by the Turner Broadcast Network in Atlanta, his life is full of work and family. Tyler's life took him out west where he currently teaches Political Science and American Government at a local community college. He's getting married this July in Vegas around the same time as our honeymoon. Brandon and I hope to crash their party. Connor announces early on he's still single and intends to stay that way.

"Do you think Chris missed his flight?" Brandon asks eagerly.

"Nope," Aiden answers while digging into the mouth-watering crab cakes we order as appetizers. "He's been here for a while. Franny and I offered him a ride, but he said he had some personal business to take care of and that he might be a little late."

"Personal business? In Tampa?" I inquire.

"Yep, that's what he said."

"I wonder what kind of personal business he needed to take care of in Tampa?" My nervous energy begins to get the best of me. Unable to slow down all my thoughts, I begin firing questions at all the guys in rapid succession. "What song did you guys pick? Did my mother okay the selection? Sierra found a place for an upright piano next to the DJ – are you okay with that, Anthony? Is Chris bringing someone to the wedding? Is that what's holding him up? Those crab cakes were amazing. Would it be weird if I ordered them for dinner, too?"

When I finish my monologue of questions and comments, Brandon and the rest of the guys just stare as if I've sprouted three heads and horn before the laughter begins and crashes through our party room with a thunderous roar.

"Damn, Scott, come up for air, little brother. I could give a shit what you order for dinner, the piano placement is fine, and we'll talk about songs and what we we're going to sing after dinner. We make all decisions together, just like the old days. Can we please just have some down time to reconnect?"

"Sorry. Wedding jitters." Looking at Brandon my heart slows to a steady pace as he grasps my hand under the table and whispers I love you. I'm overcome with emotion – privileged that this man chose me as his family. "Damn, we're getting married in two days."

Brandon never has a chance to respond as we're both caught off guard by the man of the hour. "Looks like it was meant to be." A familiar voice drags me from my intimate moment with Brandon and to the entrance of our private room. Chris. Chris is finally here.

I can barely see his face. The sun shining in from the front of the restaurant shadows his expression, but I can tell he's smiling. Slowly, carefully he takes a few steps in, and I know in an instant he's enjoying his entrance. Dressed to the nines, I'd recognize his wardrobe anywhere. I own the entire ensemble myself. A dress-down grey suit from J. Crew coupled with a light grey sweatshirt layered over a white t-shirt. Brandon's eyes are locked on what I'm sure are dsquared2 shoes and whispers while also leaving a sweet kiss near my ear, "He's alone. You can relax."

"Chris," is all that falls from my mouth as Brandon pushes back from the table extending his hand.

"Chris. Brandon Lawrence. It's good to finally meet you."

"Finally?" Chris responds while cocking his head to the left, looking quite nervous.

Recovering nicely, Brandon adds never missing a beat, "Well, you are the last to arrive. Welcome."

"Thanks. Nice to meet you as well, Brandon. All ready for your big day?"

"We've been ready for quite some time. We just needed the state of Florida to catch up with us."

Finally locating my breath and all bodily functions, I will my body out of my seat and swing one arm through Brandon's while offering Chris a quick side hug with the other. "You look good. We've all had the opportunity to catch up – you're behind. Let's get this party started."

Over the next few hours we manage to reminisce about our days together in the church choir room, the school musical theater room, and most of our shenanigans outside of both rooms. Once again, I'm surprised how comfortable I feel now that we've had a few hours together, but I notice that Chris is super quiet and lacks enthusiasm in reliving the good old days. So far he hasn't offered up much information regarding his own life, and I find it strange that no one pushes for information. Briefly, I wonder since the guys have kept in touch with each other, if he's already shared the adventures that make up his life.

Once the table is clear and the checks are settled, Anthony begins the meeting of the minds – how we always made song decisions with no pressure. My big brother is leading the charge, making sure I get a great performance from ACTS at my wedding. "First on the agenda, I'm scheduled to sing at the ceremony. Are we still good with that?"

"That hasn't changed. I wanted that from the very beginning," I smile while gazing at my soon-to-be husband.

Smiling, Anthony continues, "Song choice?"

"I have a few ideas, but I'd like to hear what you have in mind."

"For the ceremony, I would really like to sing *It's Your Love*." Brandon and I share a quick look of acknowledgement. Unable to find my voice through a myriad of emotions I simply nod at my brother. We actually considered Tim and Faith's song for our first dance. Absolutely perfect.

"I'm gonna need a little back-up. Aiden?"

"I'll need to hear the song a few times, but I'm pretty sure I know it. We'll have time to pull the arrangement together tomorrow – right?"

"Absolutely. This one calls for a little harmony. Sean?"

"I know the song well. I'm in," Sean answers with a

quick drum roll on the table.

"Okay. Now I know you two already have your first dance song. Mom said we're supposed to cover the mother/son dance and that we can pick the song. Are you good with that, or is that her idea?"

"That's what we agreed on, but . . ."

With a look of surprise Brandon studies my expression with concern. "What's on your mind, honey?"

"I was kind of thinking we could, maybe we should use the – Damn! I don't feel right asking."

Taking my hands and nodding with a smile, Brandon encourages me to answer. "You want to give the boys our song – right?"

"I'm putting you on the spot, but I know they can do it. It's been a long time, but they know the arrangement because we used to sing it all the time. Do you mind?"

"I want what you want, Scott. If they're as good as you say – why not?" I have to stop to breathe in the moment. The level of trust Brandon has in me and therefore in my old friends is staggering. Once again I feel as though I just took one more step down the aisle as our level of commitment to each other sinks in.

Smiling at my brother I'm thrilled by the prospect of the guys singing our song. "Anthony, can you guys pull the Phil Collins arrangement of True Colors together in a day? Or, do you need a karaoke track?"

"I don't know, buddy. That requires percussion and we're without instruments."

"I can cover that," Chris announces with confidence.

"Chris, thanks but I don't have room in the venue for a full drum set." Stopping to reflect, it occurs to me Chris never played an instrument. "When did you take up percussion?"

"It didn't really, but I can cover the percussion right here, from my iPad. I took up guitar in college and although I'm strictly an amateur compared to Aiden, I've been playing with another group of guys back home. All three of us play only guitar, so we stream the percussion track underneath the instruments from an app on my iPad. All we need are a few cables to connect to the sound system and we're good."

The table noise reduces to a whisper as Anthony powers through the rest of the agenda. "All that's left is the mother/son dance. Mom didn't have any special requests. What about the two of you? Brandon, seems like my little brother is getting everything he wants. Do you have any thoughts?"

"I've always been partial to the *Somewhere Over the Rainbow* mashed-up with *What a Wonderful World*. Personally, I know that's what my mother would want."

"Well, you're in luck. That's another piece we all know quite well. Aiden, I know the song from memory and can accompany but I'd much rather have you on your acoustic guitar."

"I know it well, and I play it all the time for Franny and the baby. I guess this is the reason I've been playing it so much. I've been practicing. So where are we meeting tomorrow?"

"My mother booked a small conference room on the first floor of the hotel. I looked over the space before I went to Scott's today. The piano is already there and luckily it is in tune. Let's meet by 9:00 a.m. We'll need to be at the farm for rehearsal by 6:00 p.m. Can you live without me during the day tomorrow, Scott?" My brother asks with confidence. I guess I'll need to thank my mother later on. This is a good idea. I'm so glad the boys of ACTS are here and singing at my wedding.

"Absolutely. Honestly, I don't know what to say. When mom first suggested having the boys of ACTS sing at the wedding, I wasn't sure I wanted to relive the past. I wasn't sure all of you would even come to the wedding. Now that you're here, I can't imagine getting married without the six of you singing us down the aisle." Emotionally, I'm no longer tied up in knots, just drowning with how much love I feel for everyone. When Brandon gives me a quick wink, I believe my heart does a full arabesque and I finally feel at peace with almost everything. Letting Brandon know where my head is at, I place a quick kiss to his check and begin making my way to the door of our party room. "How about a few shots to celebrate, boys? Chris, walk with me to the bar?"

"Sure."

I'm not exactly sure why I feel the need to dredge up the past, but I need to know what's going on in Chris's life. He seems happy, but very much alone. He seems excited about singing with the guys again, but yet he's so closed off he's difficult to read. At first I believed I needed this information to prepare for a family feud. My mother never mentioned he was gay, so I assume no one actually knows but me. Or at the very least the parents know nothing. There's also a part of me that wonders if he's still in hiding. Maybe he just needs a familiar face and good friend to show him the way into the light. "So, you're in Atlanta?"

"Yeah, been there about five years now. I'm working for DRH Power. I just got promoted to Vice-President of Alternative Energy Programs. We're looking into building both wind and solar fields near some of the communities south of the Atlanta airport. We'll be partnering with Siemens in Orlando, so I'll be traveling back and forth for the next couple of years."

"That's exciting, Chris. You seem very happy."

"I'm happy living far away from my family. My dad sits in judgement about everything I do. I'm not married. I haven't given him grandchildren yet. I hear it every time I visit. You know he's only here for your wedding out of some morbid hopes the wedding blows up in your face curiosity?"

"I'm sure half of our hometown believes our wedding may bring on the second coming of Christ, or that the ceremony is going to be equivalent of a three-ring circus. My parents accept my sexuality and I know they've lost some church friends because of that. It took them a while, but my family has made their peace with how I choose to live. They love Brandon. Sometimes I think my mother may love him even more than me. She refers to him as her son – the attorney."

Laughing lightly I take advantage of the pause in our conversation and order shots for the entire crew. "I'm happy for you, Scott. You are lucky. Anthony and your parents truly love you. I have to be honest, I'm a little jealous."

"I know I'm blessed." Pausing, I decide to just open Pandora's Box and see what secrets fly out. "I don't know why, but I feel like you need a friend or someone to talk to. We are friends, Chris. We've always been friends. I want to help. What's his name?"

"I'm that transparent, huh?"

"Just to Brandon and me. Not to mention, we have the same style and good taste. Nice suit, by the way. So, I have to ask. Where's your man?"

"Back home in Atlanta. We . . . Jackson and I have been together for about three years now, and we want marriage and kids, the whole package, too. Georgia will never open that door. We'll need the Supreme Court to make it happen for us. Jackson's entire family is great – very supportive. Anyway, we're not at that point yet since I'm not out to my family."

"I assumed. But three years, Chris? That's a long time to be hiding, and a tough task to boot."

"I only hide in front of my parents. I know as soon as I tell my dad, I'll probably never see them again. I'm sure I'll be banished – cast-off as some freak. Right now I can't do that to my mom. We all believed she was in the clear. Five years cancer-free and now suddenly we have something new to worry about. But as Jackson pointed out this morning, we don't actually know what we're dealing with yet. It might be nothing."

"My best advice, buddy, is to just rip off the Band-Aid. Once they know – they know. From that moment on the next move is theirs. If they choose to walk away, maybe you should let them. If you're sure Jackson is *the one* then it's time to move on with your life. Right now, you're not living at all."

"Damn, Scott, I know Jackson is it for me. I feel like I'm ready, completely settled. We just bought a house that sits on three acres about forty-five miles outside the city. I need my dad to see that we're no different than my sister and her husband. I've been looking forward to your wedding for a few months. I hope when my dad sees a marriage between two men who truly love each other, he'll loosen up on his Bible and find a way to accept I'm just a man who happens to be in love with another man." I feel bad for guy wishing he had a family more like mine. I can't wait to see my mom and dad tomorrow and to thank them for giving me the one thing every kid needs from their parents. Acceptance.

"Just curious, do the guys know about you . . . Jackson?"

"Sean does. We've gotten together several times since we both landed in Atlanta."

"Does Sean know about us?" I ask with a raised brow.

"Yeah, he does. He sort of put two and two together. And before you ask, I don't know about the rest of the guys."

"I hope I'm not overstepping here, Chris, but I'm grateful for who and what you once were to me. As far as everyone else is concerned, our past is exactly where it needs to be. In the past. Quite frankly I don't really care who knows and who doesn't. I have no regrets, no concerns, and no worries. In fact, I'd love to meet Jackson. Why don't you see if he can join us Saturday?"

"What?" At first his pause worries me. Without missing a beat he pulls out his cell phone and I can tell he's reading a text. "Are you sure?"

Out of the corner of my eye I see Brandon slide up to the bar next to me wearing a curious smile. Chris is one step away from his happily ever after and the look on his face tells me he's considering my invitation. "We're absolutely sure, Chris," Brandon replies with confidence. "Find your happiness. Find your peace, my friend. Don't you think it's about time?"

CHAPTER ELEVEN

Chris

True Colors

IND YOUR HAPPINESS. Find your peace. Don't you think it's about time?

It is. It is time. Which is exactly why two hours after those words spilled out of Brandon's mouth, I texted Jackson and asked him to join me in Tampa for the wedding of the century. His reply was simple and full of promise. "I'm on my way."

The guys and I spend most of Friday in rehearsal, and I'm amazed how well our voices still blend together. Our renditions of *True Colors* and *Somewhere Over the Rainbow* are full of emotion and will surely highlight the wedding dances. But Anthony's version of *It's Your Love* is better than good. His voice is not only powerful, but warm and comforting. I don't know why, but I believe he sings better now than he did when we were kids. Sean brings another layer to the music that offers a sweet undertone to the message of the song. I fully expect the entire crowd to find a personal message within his performance. I'm unable to hold back my thoughts and immediately question Anthony about his career choice. The entire crew piles on wondering what exactly holds him to our hometown. With a twinkle in his eye, his only response is that he'd been asking himself the same question this week.

With Scott and Brandon's blessing, I skip the rehearsal dinner and have a quiet evening with Jackson in the city. We spend the early evening strolling Tampa's Riverwalk and dining at Flambe, one of the local restaurants at Channelside Plaza. I'm not sure I'm ready to face my parents or the thousands of questions I will soon be expected to answer, but it feels right to have Jackson with me. It is time. Time to find my happiness and my peace.

My first order of business on wedding day is more rehearsal with the guys. Jackson chooses to sleep in and do a little work. Sean's wife arrived in the early morning hours and stepped in to watch our rehearsal. She couldn't keep her tears at bay. She must have voiced a thousand times how cheated she felt for not having us sing at their wedding. Before I knew it, promises were made that we wouldn't let time get in the way of our friendship ever again. I can't wait to let Jackson know we're heading to Vegas in July for Tyler's wedding.

The venue for the guys' wedding reminds me of several

farms south of Atlanta. The trees have grown undisturbed for years, leaving me almost breathless when I see the location for the ceremony. The Florida oak standing at least one hundred feet high is wrapped in rich green foliage blocking some of the afternoon sun. The trunk of the tree has been adorned with framed photos of Scott and Brandon's families and sports a hand-painted sign above signaling their family tree. Spreading out from a small white gazebo, an arrangement of at least two hundred white chairs forming a semi-circle with the tree as its center point. A twenty-foot runner of burlap lines the largest of three aisles with each side of the runner covered in soft white rose petals.

No matter which way you enter the ceremony site, a hand-painted sign welcomes guests to the wedding. A simple message of *Welcome to our Beginning* greets Jackson and me as we find seats off to the left of the gazebo. Metal buckets of white baby's breath line the outside of every other row filling the air with the sweet scent of hope. Every detail reeks of Scott's influence and careful planning.

From the moment we became entangled in our bittersweet high school affair, I knew Scott would find his way in this world. I owe him so much. Although I tried to fight it, our bond was the first honest relationship I ever had. I loved him once. And because I loved him then, I'm able to love Jackson today with all my heart. I can feel Scott and Brandon's parent's presence as well, knowing that when Jackson and I take this step we will find the same level of love and support from his family.

As the rest of the guys join us in our row, my introduction of Jackson is short, and sweet and to the point. "Guys, this is my partner, Jackson." Weirdly, not one of my friends seems shocked by my introduction or the news that I am in fact gay, only welcoming him to Tampa and the wedding of the century. I nearly chuckle out loud when it finally dawns on me, my buddies already knew and probably have for some time.

When the sound system begins to fill the air with a few familiar songs, conversations are muted as the crowd fills in all the empty chairs. Scott and Brandon are truly blessed as almost every chair is full of smiles and happy faces. Scanning the crowd I spy my parents and other hometown cronies filling in one of the back rows. Laughing out loud, I recognize they've chosen seats as far away from the nuptials in fear of some heavenly action.

When Anthony, Aiden and Sean step up to the gazebo area, the crowd quiets as Anthony's voice fills the air. When he hits the first chorus and Sean's harmony kicks in, I can't peel my eyes away from Scott's mother as her husband leads her to her seat. The gentle touch he offers the small of her back and the swift kiss he places on her lips is such a sweet gesture my heart swells. Unaware of my own actions my hand wraps with Jackson's as we continue to watch the guy's families take their walk to the gazebo.

As Anthony falls into the second verse, two delightful and beautiful little girls in the frilliest white dresses with purple sashes walk together, adding another layer of white rose petals to the burlap runner. There's a message there I think. Burlap is rough but can be quite useful. The rose petals are soft and scented and smooth. The mixture of the two reminds me that although some days may be rough, the love of your partner can only smooth the rough edges, making each step easier to take. As the girls pass our row I watch the man in front of me wrap his arm around his lady and whisper, "I am a lucky man."

My senses are so in tune with every nuance of this ceremony I find it almost difficult to manage my emotions. When Anthony begins the second chorus, Scott and Brandon join hands and walk slowly toward the gazebo. The lyrics are flooded with so much emotion, thickening Anthony's voice, preventing him from finishing the last two lines. Almost as if it were planned, Aiden pipes in with Sean to finish the song. Scott and Brandon turn toward one another, taking each other's hands before the gazebo. Before the vows begin, the entire crowd witnesses Brandon wipe Scott's tears away with one gentle touch. The beautiful lady sitting in front of me snuggles into her guy resting her head on his shoulder as he presents her with a simple white handkerchief.

Since I did not attend the rehearsal, everything I witness is real and so full of love I'm finding it difficult to hold back my own tears of joy. When Brandon's father steps up before the guys, and begins to read from the traditional marriage vows, I watch in total awe as the sun sprinkles her rays in through the limbs of the tree bathing my friends in a beautiful light. The entire crowd welcomes nature's sweet gesture.

After the traditional vows are recited and plenty of *I Dos* are announced. Scott turns to Brandon and begins his personal message.

"Life can be thought of as a series of choices. I chose to follow my heart and become the man I knew I was supposed to be. And that's why when I say I choose you, Brandon, I make that choice with a free and open heart. I love the person you are and person you make me. I know happiness in marriage isn't something that just happens. A good marriage must be created. For that reason I take you, Brandon as my best friend, my faithful partner, and my one true love. I will kill spiders for you, fill your belly with your favorite meals, kiss away all your pain, and lift you up when you are down. I promise to remember that neither one of us is perfect, but that we are in fact perfect together. I choose you Brandon Lawrence to build dreams and share my life."

Without missing a beat, Brandon leans in and kisses Scott square on the lips. "Hey, wait a minute, son, that part comes later!" His father laughs. "No cheating, son. It's your turn now." Before Brandon turns to Scott he steps up and hugs his father. No words are exchanged, but an entire message is shared between the three of them that is simply magical.

"I'm not sure how I can top that, or that I want to. Your words fill my heart with such hope for the future, I can't wait to get started. I've never felt so much . . . joy. I'm not sure I believe people fall in love. I think instead we walk into love with our eyes wide open. I believe in fate and destiny. How could I not with the way we met. And I know it is our souls that are bound together in this life and every life that came before and follows this one. For you, my love, are my soul mate. For that reason I take you, Scott, as my best friend, my faithful partner, and my one true love. I promise to pay attention to all the little things as well as the big things, to never go to sleep angry, and to stand together as we face this world. I promise you this, not with a sense of duty or sacrifice, but because you simply bring joy to my heart. I will give you whatever your heart desires, whether it's the opportunity to explore your business or to put babies in your arms. I love you means I accept you for who you are today and who you'll be tomorrow."

After exchanging rings, Brandon's father announces, "By the power vested in me by the state of Florida, and the fact that I love my boys more than life itself, I do declare they will now and will forever be Scott and Brandon Wilson-Lawrence." With nothing but cheers of happiness from the crowd the guys find a way to dance back down the aisle to a track of *This Will Be An Everlasting Love* and thunderous applause. I've attended my fair share of weddings, but Scott and Brandon's ceremony gives me such a semblance of peace I know I'm ready to live and can no longer hide.

While walking with Jackson to the back porch of the venue for cocktail hour, my father notes our joined hands and can only shake his head in disbelief. Without looking back, he and my mother walk off the grounds toward the valet stand. They choose to escape, and not face the conversation we need to have. I'm certain it will take some time before we all heal, but my healing begins today as I no longer need or want to hide.

The boys of ACTS give two monumental performances. Both mothers cry all the way through their dances with their handsome sons. But the best part of the reception is our performance of *True Colors* and how the entire crowd circled around Brandon and Scott while they shared their first dance. By the last chorus, two hundred plus voices join us as we give the happy grooms a dance they will never forget. That's the day we all showed the world our true colors.

Words do not exist to describe the moment these two wonderful human beings said I Do, I Promise, and I Love You. What I can tell you is that living in harmony is always better than living with hostility. That acceptance of people's differences is always easier than dissension, and that love always triumphs over hate.

#Lovewins

The End

Coming soon!
Julia and Josh's story continues in . . .
Shattered By Time

A SPECIAL NOTE

On June 26, 2015, in a historic 5-4 ruling, the Supreme Court of the United States found bans on marriage equality to be unconstitutional—and that the fundamental right to marriage is a fundamental right for all.

"No union is more profound than marriage, for it embodies the highest ideals of love, fidelity, devotion, sacrifice, and family. In forming a marital union, two people become something greater than once they were. As some of the petitioners in these cases demonstrate, marriage embodies a love that may endure even past death. It would misunderstand these men and women to say they disrespect the idea of marriage. Their plea is that they do respect it, respect it so deeply that they seek to find its fulfillment for themselves. Their hope is not to be condemned to live in loneliness, excluded from one of civilization's oldest institutions. They ask for equal dignity in the eyes of the law. The Constitution grants them that right." Justice Kennedy

ACKNOWLEDGEMENTS

Love wins. That's all I could think about when writing Scott and Brandon's story. Love simply wins. I was nervous to bring Scott and Brandon's story to the pages of the Time Series for fear I would never be able to capture the true essence of their relationship and do it justice. But as I began to tell their tale I discovered their love story was no different than Emma and Luke's or Mia and Isaac's or yours or mine because love simply wins.

I was halfway through writing this novella when the Supreme Court handed down their landmark decision. For the next week, every time I sat at my keyboard, I cried like a big blubbering fool.

I decided to skip the individual names for the acknowledgements this time and instead remind whoever reads these pages to be grateful for the people who love you – the family who supports you, the editor and book promoter who find every way to make you shine, the online support group that understands everything it takes to pour your heart into a story, and the friends who listen endlessly.

As writer I'm fueled by the people who surround me on a daily basis. I've been married for 31 years to the same guy. I wish I could tell you my marriage is perfect . . . but it's far from that. I am however grateful that my imperfect union is with a man who still loves me at my worst, and holds me up during my weakest moments. He is my biggest fan and greatest champion.

I consider myself a very lucky lady because the people who surround me truly root for me and for the Time Series to find success. My "tribe" is similar to the group of people who grace the pages of my books. There is a real cast of characters in my life that mirror the friendships described in each one of my stories. They read my pages, makes my covers, show up for blog takeovers, help me with research, take me to eat sushi, teach me to use chopsticks, remind me to go to yoga, ask about my family, and simply love me. Who could ask for more?

Love wins.

A Short Story Bonus – *Shadows of Time*

Shadows of Time
Tales of the Night Anthology
B.A. Dillon

Edited by Dawn Waltuck

Featuring characters
From the TIME Series

Chapter One – Grace
Tethered Through Time

Chapter Two – Brandon
It's About Time

Chapter Three – Isaac
A Vision in Time

Chapter Four – Julia
Shattered by Time (coming 2016)

Chapter Five – Emma
Tethered Through Time

Chapter Six – Scott
It's About Time

Chapter Seven – Grace
Tethered Through Time

CHAPTER ONE

Grace

"SO, EXACTLY WHERE are we heading?" My fiancé Ian asks while digging through his one and only bag.

"To be honest, I'm just following the GPS directions. I know my mom's teacher friend Scott and his husband Brandon, are hosting the Halloween party tonight, but it isn't being held at their home. The party is at some farm."

With a silly smile I can tell my man wants to play. "Scott and *his* husband?"

"Yes. His husband, you moron! You live in the United States of America now, Ian. I know it's not something you saw every day locked up in your Scottish castle, but you've been living with me for nearly three months now. Please don't play the fool. According to Mia, my mom hasn't been herself since Shane and Katie moved to Washington, D.C.

102

She's also really struggling with my brother's transfer to Denver. Grandpa Charlie, Luke and Mia pretty much insisted I get myself home this weekend to cheer up my mother."

"So, who is Scott again?"

"Scott used to be a social studies teacher at Pride Middle School where my mom works, but he's taking this year off to grow his new catering company, Amuse Bouche. You met him over a year ago at my mom's wedding. Remember?"

"Oh! He's the dude who did all the food for your mum and Luke's wedding. I remember now. The picnic basket lunches. Delicious! So, he started his own catering venture, huh?"

"Yeah. He's been incredibly busy this past year with all the weddings and parties just within our own family. My mom said he decided to take a year away from teaching to grow his business and see what happens. His husband, Brandon, is an attorney at Longfoot, Pettibone, Murphy, and Lawrence. I think the farmhouse belongs to one of their clients. I hear the house needs some TLC, but the grounds are breathtaking. The party is supposed to be in the barn."

"You think we'll be welcome since we're not in costume? This is my first American Halloween party, love. Maybe we should make a stop and at least pick up a mask or two."

"Babe, I haven't been here since I surprised mom at Mia and Isaac's adoption party. We'd be welcome if we walked in stark naked."

"Love, don't be playing with my heart like that. We're sleeping at your precious mother's home for the next four nights. As much as I'd love to shag my woman every night for the next four full moons, I'm still a little afraid of the step-dad. I only needed to be warned once. Luke Myers protects who and what his wife loves."

"Oh, Ian! You know my mother loves you. Take advantage of the down time in the car and finish your column. You have to file by Sunday – right?"

"Look at you, love. Barking orders, and I haven't even said I *do* yet."

"Don't play with me Ian Matthew O'Brien – we're seeing my big, bad step-daddy, Detective Luke Myers in about thirty minutes."

I've only been home for eight months, and the transition back to normal American life has been a breeze. I finished my tour with the United States Peace Corps back in February and quickly found my way home to Tampa. Life had surely changed there. My own father passed away during my first six months in Africa and my mother met and fell in love with Detective Luke Myers the very next year. Their beautiful romance and subsequent marriage surprised everyone but me. The first time I saw them together was magical. He is the love of her life, and that doesn't make me sad at all. Although I miss my dad, my mom is my biggest champion and deserves to be happy. And I know for a fact Luke makes my mom so very happy.

While serving in South Africa, I met and fell in love with the very funny and very freckled Ian O'Brien. Ian traveled from his mother's home in Scotland to teach English in the mountain kingdom of Lesotho as part of a delegation very similar to the Peace Corps. Our programs overlapped, and I found myself completely enthralled by the Scottish boy after one meeting. His commitment to me and the kids in his African classroom blew me away. I knew he was the real deal when he extended his tour six months just to be by my side during my remaining months in Africa. He said he was worried to leave his blonde, blue-eyed lass alone – afraid some other lad would steal my heart. He already owned my heart but I have to say I kind of like his jealous side.

Ian grew up near his mother's family in Scotland, but spent almost every summer with his paternal grandparents in Ireland. His accent confuses everyone – sometimes a thick Scottish brogue mashed up with a beautiful Irish tone. His Scottish slang is evident in his spoken language but absent from his written words. Standing six feet tall, he towers over my small frame. I have to stand on my tip-toes and he needs to bend at the knees in order to hug and kiss.

Ian's a bit of the absent-minded professor and somewhat old-fashioned, looking as though he could teach all my college classes. But his warm smile, his strawberry blonde locks, and his two-color eyes drew me in quick. His right eye is green with a warm shot of brown outlining the pupil. His left is the exact opposite, brown with the pupil surrounded by green. It's nearly impossible to look away from him once his eyes lock on mine.

At first I struggled with Ian's compulsion to constantly have skin-to-skin contact. But now, I expect to feel his hand at the small of my back, at my elbow, or wrapped around my hand everywhere we go. Even now, as I drive us away from the Tampa airport, his hand rests atop my seat and every so often his fingers jostle my hair.

When our tours were over, he was required to return to Scotland for a three month post-tour symposium. I wasn't sure if we'd survive the separation when I first returned to the states, but somehow this wonderful, loyal man found a way to make all my dreams come true. The University of Maryland welcomed me into the Master of Arts Social Work program, and through a fellowship provided by the Peace Corps, I will earn my degree in just under eighteen months. I wasn't sure how Ian would adjust to living in the states, but he tells me every day his home is with me and location is a moot point. For now we've made our home is in Baltimore, Maryland.

Due to his incredible charm, Ian was hired by Atkins Publishing to write a weekly column that appears in at least a dozen papers in the Mid-Atlantic region. He is simply brilliant, and his writing is deep and thought provoking.

"You know, love, I'm just not feeling the message this week. For the first time I may have to ask for an extension." With a shake of his head his Surface Pro is stuffed back into his bag resting on the floor of the car.

"It's been a long week, babe. Enjoy the party and I have no doubt you'll have your best column yet tomorrow."

"I love you, Gracie Finch. Don't know how I managed a day before you."

"I love you, too. According to my phone we're about fifteen minutes out. Do you need a quick refresher course on who's who?"

"Yeah. Break it down for me, love."

"Okay. Luke's dad, Grandpa Charlie, married Abby. Mia is my mom's best friend and Abby is Mia's mom. Be careful around her, babe. The lady is wicked smart and picks up on everything. She's also blind, and can't see a thing, but actually she sees through almost everything. No bullshit with her. Got it?"

"Charlie the grandad is married to the blind lady, Abby. Abby is Mia's mum, and Mia is your mum's best friend. Whoa! I'm wicked good tonight," Ian boasts through a huge smile

"Mia married Isaac. Isaac is kind of like a little brother to Luke, but they're not blood related. Charlie, Luke and Isaac are all cops – or were at one time. Clear?"

"Crystal. Isaac is like a brother and son to Luke and Charlie, but not by blood. Married to Mia, your mum's best friend, and ready to arrest me on a moment's notice."

"All of mom's friends are teachers, or were at one time. That's how Scott fits in. Remember, Scott is married to Brandon and Scott makes all the food. Compliment the food. Everyone still talks about their wedding. Their wedding was . . . there are no words. Well maybe one. Phenomenal. By the way, we're hiring his company to plan our wedding."

"Okay. Scott makes all the food, the food is great and he's married to Brandon the lawyer. We're hiring Scott to make our wedding fabulous."

"Scott's cousin, Sierra, and her husband should be there too. She's Scott's business partner and the queen at party planning. Also I think Scott's brother, Anthony, moved to Tampa over the summer. You should have heard him sing at Scott's wedding. Dreamy. His voice is smooth, velvet and rich – like a decadent piece of chocolate."

"All right. Business partner and cousin, Sierra and Scott's brother, Anthony – the wedding singer, smooth and chocolate-like. Anyone attending our age?"

"Both Sierra and Anthony are around our age and of course, Scott. He was a senior when I started high school, so he's only a few years older than me. Actually, I think he's your age."

"But he's friends with your mum?"

"Yeah, he seems older. I don't know how to explain it. Scott is friends with everyone. Julia is also a teacher at mom's school. She's . . . a little weird. Actually, she's a lot weird. I don't know the entire story, but her family is kind of freaky. She's with Isaac's brother, Josh."

"I thought Isaac was like a brother to Luke? There's an actual brother?"

"Yes. Josh is Isaac's real brother. They just reconnected last year. It's a long story."

"Gracie?"

"Yeah, babe."

"I'm not remembering any of this, you know."

"I know. But I love you for trying. And also I need you to be prepared. This is an American Halloween costume party. I expect we'll see some strange costumes tonight."

"Got it. All your mum's school chums in weird costumes. Old people in weird costumes. I'm sure I'll have no problem writing my column tomorrow."

"First off – never refer to my mom and her friends as

old. Luke would have a field day with that and you may end up arrested after all. And I'm sure you'll write a brilliant column tomorrow. I hope you're ready. This is our last turn and the house is up ahead. Ready or not . . . here we come."

CHAPTER TWO

Brandon

"BRANDON, YOU AND Scott really know how to throw a party. I haven't had this much fun in a long, long time. I feel like such a kid! I just had Luke all to myself for a private hayride," Emma giggles. "Anthony even serenaded our trip around the property." I think this is a first. Emma Myers is officially a little drunk. "Where are we by the way? Who owns this place?" She questions while attempting to find her equilibrium. Sensing his wife is a wee bit out of her element Luke slides up to her side straightening her posture and wrapping his arm around her tightly. The smile they share is one of true love. Without a doubt, this couple makes marriage look easy.

"The house and grounds belong to a client of mine. Melanie Arrow inherited this old farm house and grounds from her grandparents and she renovated most of it. The main house has a new kitchen and new bathrooms. However, the front part of the house still needs a lot of work. But now she's leaving Tampa for greener pastures. The ABC affiliate in Washington, D.C. just presented her with a contract fit for royalty. She's always coveted a spot on the news desk in the nation's capital, and my firm just made her dream a reality. I think she was packed and at the airport before the ink was dry. Melanie was so happy with the contract I negotiated she made me an offer I couldn't refuse. Scott and I wanted to host a Halloween party this year, and this weekend is Scott's and my six month anniversary. I vowed to give him whatever he wanted at our wedding. Remember?"

"I remember! I loved your ceremony, Brandon. And I remember every second of our wedding, too." Emma sighs melting into Luke's arms. "Don't you think Luke looks simply dreamy in his Danny Zuko costume?" Emma remarks while giggling. Luke is quiet and simply passes me a quick smile while leaving a sweet kiss at her temple.

"That he does! But you, gorgeous, are one fine Sandy Olsen. I think we should have a Grease dance off so you two can show us how it's done. I know Scott planned a few more party games, but let's get some dancing started."

"I just heard my name." Scott wraps his arms around me while watching Emma fall into a giggling fit. "What's so funny, Emma? Are you messing with one of my best girls, honey?" My handsome husband inquires.

"Not at all, Scott. I think the very sensible and very predictable Emma Myers has had one too many Jello shots, dear."

"I would tend to agree. I think before we move onto party games or dancing, I need to hydrate my wife and get a couple of ibuprofen in her stat," Luke states in his typical, very sensible tone.

"If you head out the side barn door, follow the cobblestone steps up to the back door. The mud room leads into the kitchen. I left a bottle of pain reliever on the counter after I saw the sheer number of Jello shots my wonderful husband made. I assumed someone would need them tonight."

"You are well prepared, counselor." Turning to his giggling wife, Luke's grasp is firm but tender. "Let's head up to the main house for a few, sweetheart."

"So, what was that all about? In all the years I've known Emma, I've never seen her out-of-control before," Scott mentions while watching Luke guide Emma through the barn. Before I have a chance to answer Rebecca, Julia, and Mia come in search of Scott.

"Emma's a little down in the dumps. She misses Katie, Shane and baby Lucy. We all do," Mia mentions with fresh tears in her eyes. For a moment the lack of conversation makes me a tad uneasy, but Julia always finds a way to clearly state the obvious.

"You all know as well as I do, Emma's a little bummed out. Shane's transfer to FBI headquarters in Washington, D.C. caught us all off guard. But I think KJ's promotion and transfer to Denver is the straw that broke the camel's back," Julia states with a warm smile. Both Scott and I are thrilled with her transformation. She finally has put all her ghosts to bed and seems herself once more. Julia and Josh are a riot together, and I'm glad she is finally settled.

While slipping his arm around my back, Scott offers another piece to the puzzle. "I'm sure KJ's decision to call off his wedding didn't help either. Does anyone know when we should expect Grace and Ian? That will put a permanent smile on Emma's lovely face."

"They landed about an hour ago. Emma will be fine once she sees her baby girl. Give her a couple of days to come to terms with the distance she now shares with her kids. She'll be fine, Luke will make sure she has everything she needs." Mia answers with a sweet smile.

All of our friends from both Pride Middle and my firm have made an appearance at our very first Wilson-Lawrence Halloween costume party. Julia and Josh swooped in as Batman and a very sexy Catwoman. Emma and Luke look absolutely adorable as the leading couple of Grease – Danny Zuko and the sweet Sandy Olsen. But the award for over-the-top sexy has to go to Mia Miller. Dressed in the sexiest cop uniform on the planet, her bare midriff even has me skating my eyes over her well-toned body. In all the years I've known him, Isaac is always dressed to the nines. But tonight he's covered in black and white stripes, forever the jailbird. I suspect Mia's been kind, handcuffing his arms in front. When I catch him watching me, his look clearly states to take my eyes off his woman. No worries, Detective Miller. I married the love of my life and I'm gay – but I'm not dead. Mia Miller is drop-dead gorgeous.

I ordered, or rather strongly suggested that Scott and Sierra put the business aside for this party, and asked everyone to bring a dish to share. Tonight we have a virtual smorgasbord of food. Everyone showed up with at least two dishes, one for the main table and of course one for the dessert wars that always find a way into our gatherings. My husband's new, autumn cupcake creations are fantastic, but I have to give this one to Emma. Her candy-corn ice cream served overtop Katie's chocolate brownie recipe has everyone making return trips to the dessert table.

My sister Evie and her husband along with my co-workers are also here tonight for a change of pace. My favorite part of the night so far is the pumpkin carving contest we organized to start off the festivities. Scott's idea, of course. My secretary, Miriam, laughed for days at Scott and Sierra's beautiful invitations and the final message of B.Y.O.P. Miriam had to explain 'Bring Your Own Pumpkin' to our managing partner Floyd Pettibone and senior partner, Paul Longfoot. Taking a full ninety minutes, the entire crew, along with even old Paul and Floyd, worked furiously creating a few interesting designs. For now, eighteen carved pumpkins, lit to perfection, line one wall of the barn. Everyone has been encouraged to examine all the bright orange creations and vote for their favorite. Scott has packaged a dozen of his cupcakes for the artists of the winning carved creation. But my husband, armed with his usual competitive spirit, has ours sporting an entire scene. I don't know how we did it, but our spooky ghost face looks so real, even I have to give it a double-take. Wait a minute! What was that? Was someone just standing behind the pumpkin table?

"Honey, you promised there weren't any critters living

in this barn!" Scott exclaims while beginning the first of one of his many host meltdowns I expect to see tonight.

"Scott, Melanie assured me this barn has been animal free for some time. What's the problem?"

"I've replaced the serving spoon on the chili twice already, and now it's gone again. Mia just put out a plate of hors d'oeuvres including the little bacon-wrapped hotdog weenies I love so much. Now there's a trail of food leading to the back of the barn to all those bales of hay you said we didn't have to worry about. Don't get me started on desserts. Emma said she made six dozen cookies, and there's only crumbs left on the plate. Some critter's having the feast of his life in this barn, and we have more than thirty people to feed!"

"Babe, Scott, look at all the food over there. Believe me no one's going hungry here tonight, honey. There's probably a few stray cats that helped themselves to your hotdog weenies, and the serving spoons were probably left aside another dish. As far as the cookies go, I've seen Luke, Isaac, and Josh at the dessert table several times tonight. Believe me, those boys ate the cookies, Scott."

"I'm not putting any more food out until Grace and Ian arrive. Maybe we should move the tables forward and away from the bales of hay?"

"Let's do that. Did anyone use real candles in their pumpkins?" I ask now concerned that our invaders could cause some real trouble.

"No. Everyone used the same small battery operated light I provided. Why?"

Before I can answer, squeals of joy and laughter draw both Scott and I away from the pumpkins to the entrance of the barn as we find the very lovely Emma Myers wrapped around her beautiful daughter, Grace. Standing somewhat perplexed next to Grace is her fiancé, Ian, laughing lightly as he scans the crowd. "Oh my God! Grace! Ian! Did you all know about this?" Emma croons with tears of joy. This family is something to behold. Grace and poor Ian are passed around through the crowd like a sparkly new toy on Christmas morning. When Ian's eyes land on me, he steps up to shake my hand.

"Scott?"

"Nope, his husband, Brandon. Welcome, Ian. We're so glad you're here."

"Nice costume. Walking Dead?"

"Yep. Yours?"

"Scottish boy trying to understand American culture."

"Works." Before we can continue Grace makes her way to Ian's side and offers me a quick hug. "Welcome, beautiful girl. I hope you're hungry? There's enough food here to feed a small army."

"Yeah, we didn't have time to grab anything after we landed. Thanks," Grace responds with a furrowed brow. "I thought this was an adult only party, Brandon? Mia and Isaac couldn't find a babysitter?"

"Huh?"

"Who brought their kids?"

"What kids?"

"The kids who just helped themselves to about six cupcakes on the dessert table two seconds ago."

"Grace, no one brought their kids tonight."

"Hmmmm. Well then, either I'm seeing things, or you all have a few party crashers tonight."

CHAPTER THREE

Isaac

"**B**ABE, ARE YOU okay? You look a little green around the edges," I mention as Mia downs another bottle of water.

"Yeah, just feel really dehydrated today so I've been drinking a ton of water tonight. I have to pee again. I'm just running up to the house for a few minutes. I'll be right back."

When my gorgeous wife Mia slips out through the side barn door I find it hard to believe how much my life has changed this year. My world is only about my girls, Mia and our two beautiful angels, Sarah and Sophie. Sarah was a little uncomfortable with Mia's sexy cop costume when we prepared to leave tonight, but our youngest only had compliments. 'Mommy is beautiful' she said to me over and over – and I couldn't agree more. During our private hayride all

I could think about was finding the two of us some privacy and having her arrest me one more time tonight. The short shorts, her bare midriff, and black high heeled boots have me casing the entire joint for a private room.

But now, I'm worried she's coming down with something. She needed a nap this afternoon in order to prepare for tonight, and now it looks like she had one too many green Jello shots or Julia's Smokin' Hot Chili did a number on her smokin' hot body. I glance around the party and think maybe I should take her home.

"Where's your wife, little brother?" It's difficult to take anything Josh says serious tonight dressed as the Caped Crusader.

"Bathroom. Where's your Catwoman, Batman?" I ask watching the door for Mia's return.

"Dancing with Scott and rest of the kids."

"What kids?"

"You know, Scott, Brandon, Sierra, Anthony, Grace, and Ian – the kids! I don't know this music. I feel old. Do you think I'm too old for her, Isaac?"

"Julia?"

"Yes, Julia. Who'd you think I was asking about? Look at her." Julia is having the time of her life dancing, but her eyes are on Josh the entire time. "The idea of having to dance to this shit ranks right up there with having my guts ripped out by the Walking Dead folks already on the dance floor."

"I never thought I'd see the day," I laugh while shaking my head.

"See what day?"

"The day when my over-confident, talented at every-thing big brother has a moment of weakness. Julia is like my age, Josh. You're only eight years older than me. Why are you suddenly worried about age?" I'm so taken by this moment of weakness, I'm not exactly sure what to say or do next. I watch him watch Julia and it suddenly dawns on me where he's headed. "Wait. Are you in love with Julia?"

"Without a doubt."

"Have you told her that?" I ask with surprise etched into my question.

"Several times."

"Does she feel the same way?"

"She does," he answers with a timid smile.

Laughing, I have to ask. "So what the hell are you whining about?"

"I can't dance."

"No one can dance to this shit, brother."

"They're dancing."

"No, there moving around to some shitty-ass music. Go ask Anthony to put on some classics. I'd like to get these handcuffs off and wrap my arms around my beautiful wife for a song or two."

"I'm on it. Thanks, bro." Josh shoots through the crowd with ease and has a very brief conversation with our new friend, Anthony. Within minutes, the boss-man himself comes blaring through the speakers. Just what we needed – some old-time rock and roll.

When Mia returns, she looks as though whatever had ahold of her finally let go, and she's wearing the silliest smile.

It's almost disarming. As we head to the center of the barn to dance, Mia and Emma share a secretive smirk and wink that has me wondering if the two of them are up to something. Emma and Mia together are one dangerous pair of smart, sexy women.

"Do you want something to drink, babe? The lawyers hauled in about two dozen bottles of wine. There's some good stuff over there."

"Nah, not really in the mood for a drink, but wouldn't mind laying you out in the back of that wagon. Anthony said all the hayrides were over." She whispers with a sexy smile and a traveling tongue over the shell of my ear. It's a wonder I can still stand up.

"Babe, you must be reading my mind! Think we can duck out of here unnoticed for a few?" Not waiting for an answer, my hand grips hers in an instant and we are on the move.

With the music still playing, and most of the crowd settled around and catching up with Grace and Ian, no one notices as we slip out the main door. It's a bewitching night in Tampa. The harvest moon, sits high, lighting up the property. The sky is clear and there are thousands of twinkling stars overhead. Scott and his party crew added a thousand more twinkling lights along the fence showcasing the grounds a little more than I would like. I notice the fire pit is readied and I'm hoping that means S'mores are in my future. Mia and I walk hand in hand toward the wagon, but I suddenly feel the urge to stop, bring her in close and kiss her under the moonlit sky.

"Wow. I love you. What was that for?" The next thing I know she's snuggled into my side and finishes with a loud sigh.

"I love you, so much, Mia. There are times I feel the need to check-in and make sure I'm not dreaming. You and the girls are my greatest gift."

"Okay handsome, I love you more than I can say. Not only is our life real, the reality is we are rarely without kids. As much as I love you and the sentiment you just described, I really just want you for your body tonight. I'm not sure what's going on, but I'm horny as hell."

"Oh, babe, I like the way you think. Grab that blanket and let's get you –" Stopping to step my body in front of my wife I look to the side of the barn and focus on two small figures scamper toward the main house. "Did you see that?"

"Yeah. Probably just one of the younger kids from Brandon's firm heading up to the main house. Stop worrying and let's go get naked in the wagon, Detective Myers."

"It's just – they looked like kids. Like Sarah or Sophie's age," I offer with a furrowed brow. Something feels off.

"Honey, our kids are fine. We have a great sitter. We checked in with her several times tonight. Charlie said he and my mom are leaving around ten, so they'll be home soon and nearby before long. Stop worrying and let's go get naked. Besides, in addition to the few tricks I have up my sleeve, I also have a little treat in store for you tonight. There's something I need to tell you."

Completely distracted by my very sexy wife, all I can think about is an hour of alone time in the back of the wagon. "Kids? What kids? Are three blankets enough? Leading my wife to the wagon, it's time to transfer these handcuffs to her wrists for the next hour. "I intend to have you naked and writhing beneath me for the next hour, Mrs. Miller. How's that for tricks and treats?"

CHAPTER FOUR

Julia

"**O**KAY. WHAT'S WRONG, Josh? You've been pouting for the last hour. Are you sad I didn't dress up as your Robin?" I ask while wrapping my arms around his middle.

"What? I'm not pouting. And no, not sad about the Robin thing at all! You will always be my Catwoman, babe." He smiles while planting a sweet kiss at my temple.

"So, what's wrong?

"I just feel . . . I feel old here tonight, Julia. For the first time in my life, I know I'm one of the 'older guys' at the party. I don't recognize any of the music, and the entire Surface Pro versus Apple Macbook discussion you were having with Ian and Scott was way over my head. It's like I just crossed over some imaginary line into another generation."

"Josh, you are far from old. You're way too hot to even

124

think about the word old. In fact all the young girls from Brandon's firm were talking about how much you look like Scott Eastwood. I wanted to be jealous, but instead I just yelled – Hell YES! And he's with me ladies. Hands off!"

"Who's Scott Eastwood?"

"Clint Eastwood's son. He's hot and all over all the internet these days. But he's got nothing on you! You are the entire package, hon. Have I mentioned how grateful I am for everything you are to me, and what you went through to get us to this point? I love you."

"I love you, too, Julia. You know that, right?" When his hands gently grasp my cheeks I know what's next. One of his make me shiver, hot as hell, take me any way he can get me kisses. And I'm not disappointed or embarrassed when he puts his tongue in my mouth, and all my friends have a front row seat to our very public display of affection.

Letting out a full breath, I can feel my toes curl in my boots as he douses me with a series of short butterfly kisses all over my face. This boy knows exactly what to do with his lips and tongue every single time. "I know you love me. But this is all new territory for me, Batman. The longest relationship I had before you lasted maybe a month. Please be patient with me." My voice is barely a whisper. I'm not sure if Josh truly appreciates how far I've come and how far I still need to travel. I'm left feeling somewhat lost and reply with a return kiss that begs for patience and understanding.

Reading my emotions and the plea from my kiss he answers in the only way he knows how. Change the subject and add a shot of humor. "I can be patient. But can we leave now? I'd like to get you back to the Batcave and have my way with you several times tonight, Catwoman."

"We can't just leave without checking in with everyone and saying good-night. Come on now, Batman, let's be adventurous and find a secluded spot right here," I purr right at his mouth.

"I love the way you think, Catwoman! How 'bout I lay you out in the back of my truck under the stars? I bet there's something in my utility belt I can use to restrain you." The pure want and need in his voice has me practically climbing his body as he directs our movement outside.

Before I have a chance to verbalize a comeback, we've stepped behind the barn to where everyone parked their cars tonight, and head toward Josh's F-150. The night sky is beautiful, blanketed with twinkling stars and a full harvest moon that puts the capital "R" in romance. There's some irony here, as we are quite the pair. Inside the barn we could barely keep our hands in respectable places, and I nearly devoured him during our last kiss. But outside, romance encapsulates the moment and tones down the raw sexual tension. Josh's hand wraps around mine while our arms swing loosely as we stroll toward the truck. At this point there's no need for words. I know how much he loves me, and what I have to lose if I screw this up.

"We were in such a hurry to get out here I didn't think this plan all the way through, babe. Let me get you settled in the bed of the truck and I'm gonna run back to the barn and grab a couple of blankets and a bottle of wine."

"Better grab two bottles, Batman. We may be here a

while," I whisper while removing my first boot.

I have to chuckle as my last response sends Josh jogging along the path we just strolled, and back inside the barn. Tonight has been so much fun. The weather is ideal, and the night sky is crystal clear. Thinking of everyone in costume causes a slight giggle to fall from my lips. All my friends, this extended, blended family is happy and living the dream. My giggle gives way to loud sigh and relaxes my body into one big pile of sappy goo.

Surveying the grounds I can't help but wonder why Brandon picked this location to host the party tonight. The property is gorgeous and must cover a minimum of fifty acres. Thanks to our beautiful Florida weather, the rose garden to the east of the house still boasts countless blooms in multiple colors, and the path that leads to the main house is lined with buckets of yellow chrysanthemums and orange marigolds.

When I first see her walking from the rose garden toward the truck I feel like my eyes are playing tricks with my mind. Who is that? I don't remember seeing her inside the barn. A young woman, probably from Brandon's firm, and dressed similarly to Brandon, Scott and the rest of the Walking Dead crowd picks up her pace as she heads my way wearing a frenzied look.

"Hi!" I call out with concern. "Hey, are you okay?"

"I don't know," she answers while her eyes skate back and forth over the acreage.

"What's your name, sweetheart? Do you work with Brandon at the firm?"

"What? Brandon? Who?" She inquires with a dull, lifeless look.

"Oh, honey . . . you're not a guest at this party, are you? What's your name, sweetheart? Are you hurt?"

"Irene. My name is Irene. My kids? Are they safe now?" She begs with wide eyes.

"I haven't seen any kids. Irene, honey, what happened to you?"

"I need to find them!" She shrieks while pacing in front of me. "Please help me, Julia."

"Of course. Let me get my boots back on. I'll help you." Shit! She knows my name. For just a moment my heart stops and I think I forget to breathe. Not wanting to upset her any further I decide a calm demeanor is best and to mention the cops inside the barn. "I'll gather the rest of the troops to help. Several of the party guests are cops. We'll find your babies, Irene." When I look up to jump from the truck bed Irene has vanished. Vanished into thin air and there's no sign of her anywhere. I only turned my head for ten seconds while pulling on my boot. What the hell is going on?

Scanning the property, I look toward the barn entrance and watch with trepidation. My heart is racing, practically beating out of my chest. Oh God! What was that? Who was that? I'm somewhat relieved as I watch Josh exit the side barn door carrying several blankets and couple of bottles of wine. But my breath stops completely when I witness Irene's frame pass directly through Josh's body and into the barn.

"Holy hell, she most definitely does not work at Brandon's firm." I mutter to myself while shaking my head. As I begin my quick pace toward the barn, the realization of what just transpired fully settles into my overloaded brain. First, the booty call in the back of Josh's truck will have to wait for another day. And finally, my days of seeing and talking to dead people are definitely not over.

CHAPTER FIVE

Emma

"**P**ROMISE ME. PROMISE that you'll always cut me off after two drinks! I'm a bit humiliated, Luke. What came over me tonight, honey? I never drink like that." My cheeks still feel flushed but thanks to Luke's earlier intervention, a hangover isn't in my future.

Melting into my husband's side, my world is righted once again as his strong arms wrap around my middle. "Well . . . to be honest, you really didn't drink. I don't think you understand the concept of a 'Jello shot.' Emma, that's pure Vodka. Sweetheart, we all know you're struggling a little bit. It's really okay. Everyone understands."

"Honey, I'm not struggling a little bit. I'm struggling a lot. Having the kids and Katie so far away now just feels weird. I feel so lost."

"I know. I can't tell you how many times I pick up the phone to text Shane, or walk to the next office expecting to find him there. So, I get it. But, Emma remember, we can get on a plane anytime you feel the need to see KJ, Grace, or Katie and the baby. We'll visit. They'll visit. I'm sure we'll see them all the time. Besides, KJ's transfer to Denver is just temporary. I'm sure he'll land back in Orlando. The company headquarters is there."

"Or Copenhagen. The headquarters for his division is in Copenhagen, Denmark. He's already talking about a trip there soon."

"Sweetheart, let's not go there now. How did you manage when Grace was in Africa for two years?"

"I saw her twice. I knew there was an end date. I don't know – I met you. I was distracted. Oh honey, I just miss my babies," I whisper as my tears begin to flow once again. Over the past two years, I've come to rely on one constant. Luke Myers. When I'm feeling somber or blue his arms immediately circle around me – chasing away the darkness. So when my husband's arms fall from around my waist instead, a shiver runs down my spine that leaves me cold and empty. Not the reaction I've come to expect from my fabulous husband. I'm so accustomed to his desire to dote on my every need, a small corner of my brain or maybe even my heart feels a bit disappointed.

When I finally lift my eyes, the first thing I notice is Luke Myers, doting husband has been replaced by Luke Myers, former police detective and now FBI agent. Luke has stepped away and he and Isaac are in the middle of what appears to be a serious conversation. Before I know it, they are joined by both Josh and Charlie and the conversation shifts further away as I strain to hear the news of the hour.

"What's going on, Mom?"

"I don't know, sweetie. Probably some case they're working on. Are you having fun?"

"A blast. You look like you're . . . sorry you ever swallowed a Jello shot?"

"You can say that again. Jello shots are a one-time deal for this lady!" Without warning Grace and I are pulled from our conversation as Mia and Julia wave us over to the dessert table.

"Mia, where have you been? You're covered in straw and it's matted in your hair and –" I stop abruptly knowing she literally must have just had a roll in the hay. Lucky girl!

"We were interrupted by Isaac's ringing cell phone. Some days I want to chuck that device right down the toilet." Brushing my hands down her back I quickly try to remove all the evidence that supports a recent roll in the hay.

"Sorry, hon. But when I told Josh about Irene and then Gracie mentioned the kids at the dessert table we decided we needed Isaac. Something weird is going on here tonight." Before any one of us knows what to say, Julia begins loading her plate with multiple desserts. The girl eats like every guy I know and doesn't gain a pound. I secretly hate her a little. "Sorry, Mia. Next weekend Uncle Josh and I will babysit so you and Isaac can finish your sexy time."

Mia's response is simply an eye-roll in Julia's direction and wink in mine. I mouth quickly to Mia, "did you tell him?"

And am met with a quick negative shake of the head while she continues to pull straw from her curly brown locks. But now I'm confused. Who's Irene? Kids at the dessert table? And why is this interrupting everyone's evening? There aren't any kids here. This is an adult-only party. "Who's Irene, Julia? Inquiring minds want to know."

"The spirit I met outside. Her kids are missing," Julia mentions in passing while getting ready to bite into one of Scott's cupcake creations.

"The what?" I ask without much emotion. When Mia calmly recounts Julia's encounter with Irene, the three of us discuss the event as if we're talking about the weather.

"Stop! Wait a minute," Gracie interjects. "Julia saw a spirit? Like an actual ghost of someone who is dead? Mom? Mia? Why are you both so calm? You both act as if this is something you deal with every day."

"Honey, some things have happened around here the past two years that —"

"What things? To you? All three of you?" This is exactly why we do not share our spiritual connections outside this group. Without the experience, most people just cannot accept the unknown.

"You see . . . things of a spiritual nature tend to gravitate toward the three of us."

"What are you talking about?" Grace's emotions are getting the best of her, but I'm certainly not ready for mainstream America to meet Julia, the ghost whisperer and Mia, the visionary. I don't know what to call my experience except something purely out of this realm.

"Grace . . . we like to keep our experiences somewhat private. Honey, please lower your voice. Can you do that?" Nodding, Grace's arm wraps around my back as the three of us pull her in close for a few private revelations. "Well, at times Mia can see beyond the here and now. She has a gift, honey. She has full blown visions that describe either a past event or something that may happen in the future. Sometimes she even sees in real time – as an event is happening. Gracie, about two years ago one of Mia's visions saved Luke's life." I pause briefly and give her a moment to let the memories of Luke's undercover work sink in.

"I honestly don't know what to say. What's your role in all of this, Mom?"

"Gracie, honey, that story will have to wait for another day. Luke and I really want tell you all about that. Together. But we'll need a couple of hours. Long story. An interesting story, but a long one."

"I suppose next you're gonna tell me Julia sees and talks to dead people."

"Honey . . . as a matter of fact, yes. Julia's a medium of sorts. But all of this is very new to her, and it would really help if you didn't look at us like we're all a bunch of loons." My request is simple but sincere. Grace's reaction is to study my expression as her head fills with numerous questions.

"Mom? I don't know what to say. Damn, what am I supposed to tell Ian? Wait – I know. The spirit world has invaded Tampa. Mia can predict the future, Julia talks to dead people, and my Mom's keeping her story locked up tight right now." Her sarcasm bites, but is understandable. To those on the outside of our ghostly experiences, we sound nothing but crazy.

"Gracie, I know this is all a little hard to swallow. We've had the last two years to get used to all the weird episodes flocking in our direction – nothing shocks us anymore. The guys – they're used to it as well. At any rate, the girls say you saw kids when you and Ian first arrived tonight?"

"Yeah. I was hugging Brandon when I saw three kids by the dessert table. I mentioned it to him, but he said there weren't kids here. But I saw them as clear as I see you right now. The oldest girl was holding a toddler and the little boy lifted about six cupcakes before they disappeared behind the bales of hay." Grace's demeanor relaxes as we continue to bring her up to speed on the adventures of the past two years.

"Luke, Josh and Isaac need to know what you saw." Looking in Mia's direction, I give the best advice I can muster. "You, both of you need to tell Isaac what's going on." Mia only has smiles for my advice and offers me a celebratory wink.

"Sure, Mom. If you think it's really necessary. I didn't see much though."

"I don't know why but I'd bet the mortgage the kids you saw are the kids Irene is looking for. You need to give the guys a detailed description, honey."

"Wait," Julia directs with an outstretched hand. "How old do you think the kids were, Grace?"

"Hmmm, the little one is no more than two. The oldest might be ten, but I'm not sure. The little boy is somewhere in-between. Why?"

"Irene is just a kid herself. I doubt she's their mother. I wonder if she's an older sister or something?" Julia whispers while scanning the barn.

Before we all have a chance to touch base with the guys, Scott steps up to the karaoke mic and announces Floyd Pettibone and his wife the winner of the pumpkin carving contest. The winning design – a traditional, smiling, toothy jack-o-lantern. With thunderous applause Scott reaches for the winning creation only to be met by the smile of a toothy young boy hiding behind the table. With wide eyes, he looks down each side of the table for a possible escape route, but pauses instead as Scott reaches for his hand. The two, Scott and our young invader, share a private moment until Scott encourages him to come out of his hiding place. Holding firmly onto a few of Scott's long fingers, our young guest is obviously overwhelmed by the silenced crowd and staring eyes.

Without missing a beat and a nod in Scott's direction, I encourage the party to continue as I make my way to Scott's side. I spend so many days talking to kids, this moment is meant for me. As a school counselor, all the guys encourage me to take the lead. Kneeling down to the little lad's height I offer a smile and a tousle of his hair. "Hi there. My name's Emma. What's your name, little man?"

"Connor," he answers shyly.

"Please don't be afraid, Connor. We all just want to help you, buddy. Do you think Scott and I could walk you up to the main house away from the big crowd? That way we can talk and maybe get you cleaned up a bit." Before I have a chance to continue, I watch the little guy examine Scott from head to toe. It's odd, he doesn't seem nervous at all and feels incredibly safe holding onto Scott's hand. Their immediate bond warms my heart.

Studying Scott's sweet smile he mutters out a quick answer. "Okay. Can my sisters come, too?"

Expecting more kids due to Grace's earlier description I'm able to answer without surprise. "Of course they can," I offer with a wide smile. "Where are they?"

Looking at Scott, Connor's nerves seem to melt away as his next words are meant only for him. "You make really great cupcakes, sir." A bit of laughter falls from the small crowd as I watch Scott unable to pull his gaze away from the young boy. "I'm sorry we took so many, but they tasted so yummy and made my stomach stop growling." As Connor continues his very long apology for the missing food, Isaac and I manage to coax out an older girl carrying a small toddler from behind the large bales of hay. Like Connor, both girls are covered in filth as it becomes quite obvious to all they've been hiding here for some time.

"Hi, love. My name is Emma. Can you tell me your name, sweetheart?" I ask as the young girl straightens her shoulders and lifts her chin ready to protect her siblings. "Honey, I promise. No one here wants to hurt you. This is my friend, Isaac. He's a policeman, love. We just want to help." As I finish my speech tears begin to roll down her cheeks as she begins to loosen her grip on the small child in her arms. It's obvious, she's been caring for both Connor and the toddler during their time in the barn. Without missing a beat, Brandon steps up and takes the squirming toddler from her arms.

"My name is Sam. Samantha." Looking at the toddler with a sweet smile, her voice is almost muted by the tears continuing to flow. "That's my baby sister, Isabella."

"It's so nice to meet you, Sam. I was just asking your brother if we could head up to the main house so we can talk. I'd like to get to know you better and I think you might be more comfortable away from the big crowd. Several of those nice guys right there are policeman and they just want to help. How does that sound?"

Hardening quickly, Sam removes little Isabella from Brandon's arms, and calls Connor to her side. With a firm stance and a falling smile she begins to negotiate a safe place. I've seen it a handful of times, and know immediately what we are dealing with. These kids are running from a horrific situation. More than likely an unsafe home. "Can we just stay here – with you?" She pleads while looking directly at Scott and Brandon. Even though I've done most of the talking and introduced the guys as cops these kids only seem to feel safe with Scott and Brandon.

"Honey, l promise Emma and Isaac only want to help you. If it helps, Scott and I will stay close," Brandon offers to quell the brewing storm.

Sam's reaction is to huddle her siblings in close and nod in Brandon's direction. "Okay. But just so we're clear – we won't go back there! Make sure the policemen know we can't go back there!"

CHAPTER SIX

Scott

ONNOR'S LITTLE HAND won't let go of mine. I can't
let go of his.

Isabella is in love with my husband. For the record, Brandon's head over heels in love with this little angel
as well. He looks good with a baby in his arms.

Samantha . . . Sam is scared to death, but for some reason she continues to watch the two of us closely. At first I
thought it was only because we are holding her siblings. But
it feels like there's more. She trusts the two of us for some
unknown reason.

Isaac's phone call that interrupted our evening was
from his partner. Helicopters were in our area looking for
three runaways. Three kids who had run away from a foster home approximately five miles west of Melanie Arrow's
farmhouse.

It appears a Department of Children and Family social worker, checking in on five wards of state, was denied entrance by the foster parents, Max and Janelle Anderson earlier today. When sheriff deputies arrived, they too were denied entrance into the home. An FBI Child Protective task force, designed in part by one Luke Myers, was called in to help remove the children from the Anderson home. When the task force finally gained entry, they found one dead teenage girl, another teen barely breathing and three missing children. Irene Martin, 16, was found dead in one of the bedrooms. Her twin brother, Mac, was helicoptered to St. Joseph's Children's Hospital. His condition at this time is unknown. The three missing children are now our guests in the main house as we wait for local deputies and an agency social worker. The Andersons – arrested, and charged with Irene's murder.

"Connor? How about you and me head into the bathroom to wash up a bit?" I don't know why, but my young friend agrees refusing to let go of my hand. We spend the next fifteen minutes in comfortable silence. I scrub off my Walking Dead face as he scrubs off the filth from living in that house. Soon Samantha, Brandon, and baby Isabella join us. Samantha and Brandon remove all of Isabella's torn clothes and give her a full bath. I can't even describe the water. After thirty minutes, Brandon and I look like the living, but the kids have erased only half of the dirt they've been living in. Somehow Julia and Josh skipped out to a local Walmart and return with diapers and clean clothes for all three kids. When Samantha sees the new clothes she returns to the bathroom to take a full shower. Connor follows. Samantha and Connor say very little. They are so quiet. Almost too quiet.

"Mr. Scott?" Samantha whispers while running her fingers through her wet, long, blonde hair. Her tears flow freely as I'm sure she's questioning what's next for her and her siblings.

"Yes, sweetheart. Do you need something?" What a ridiculous question. She needs parents who love her. Real parents and a home. Stylish clothes, and lots of good food.

"Is there anyway . . . anyway at all we could just stay here with you and Mr. Brandon for a few nights? I just need a good night's sleep. I know I could sleep here. I just need a few nights, and then I'll be okay to look after Connor and Isabella. We watched the two of you get ready for your party today. We like you. We trust you." Oh. My. God. I want to wrap my arms around this precious angel and never let go. I don't know where to begin. First, not my house. Second, the foster care system. Can you say red-tape nightmare?

"Samantha, I'm not sure --" Dropping my head into my hands, I can't find the words. Where is my husband? Where is Emma? Need some help here, people, I voice to no one.

"Scott, mind if I take this one?" Brandon offers with his smooth smile. I nod quickly in his direction and begin running a comb through Sam's blonde locks. "Sam, your social worker is here."

"Oh." She mumbles trying to hide her emotions.

"She needs to ask you a few questions. Mr. Scott and I have been thinking about starting a family for a long time. A few months back we filled out all kinds of legal documents, and we are approved foster care parents pending we find a larger home." Forgot all about that. We pushed pause on the adoption process while I worked on growing my catering business. "I talked with your social worker, and the state is going to allow the three of you to stay with us for the next few weeks. Temporarily, they are making Scott and I your foster parents . . . but only if you're okay that. We know you've been through so much. No pressure, sweetheart."

Showcasing her first smile, the following two words bring on my own waterworks. "Yes, please," she whispers.

"Sweetie, your social worker wants to talk with you and Connor in the kitchen, and I need to bring Scott up to speed on everything we need to do." With hugs for both of us Samantha hastily makes her way out of the bathroom. "Let's chat in the mudroom, Scott."

Still unable to find any words, Brandon guides me toward the mudroom and then outside to the back steps. The music still blares from the barn reminding me we still have guests. My head is spinning a million miles per hour. I have guests in the barn and three kids in the kitchen. I think *I have* three kids.

Finally finding my voice, I mention my biggest concern. "Umm, Brandon, honey? Does the nice social worker lady know our condo only has two bedrooms?"

"Yes. And she also knows that *our* house . . . *this* house has four bedrooms."

"What? This house? Our house?" I have guests in *my barn*, and three kids in *my kitchen*. My kitchen?

"Scott, before she left for D.C., Melanie offered to sell me her family home. She was so happy with her new contract and loves the big city. She wants to sell, and she wants to sell this place to us. The first time I walked into this house, I knew it was meant for us. The grounds can become your catering venue, the kitchen is perfect for your business and a family. And most importantly, the house is big enough for our family to grow. What do you say? Want to buy a farm and start a family?"

"Is this a joke, Brandon Wilson-Lawrence? Because if you're playing with me, you're gonna be part of the real Walking Dead!"

"No tricks, babe. I only offer treats tonight. Happy Halloween!"

CHAPTER SEVEN

Grace

(The next day)

"**G**RACIE! YOU AND Ian need to get moving. We're leaving in five minutes!" My mother is forever hurrying me along. I miss her every day – except for her constant nagging about tardiness. Makes me feel like I'm back in middle school. Luke says he appreciates her tardy bells, that he's never late and always on time.

We've been on the go since the sun came up today. Mom and I whipped up a breakfast fit for royalty. I've never seen Ian eat that many pancakes in one sitting. Afterward, my mom and Luke shared their story with the two of us. She was right, it's a long one, and it took nearly two hours to tell. To say I'm shocked is an understatement. I'm not sure I will ever completely understand their special connection. I've never given any thought to the idea of past lives before. But after the story my mom and Luke shared today, I will most definitely be reading up on the topic. I was worried what Ian would think of the mystical realm invading my family, but his reaction was stellar. His only comment after they finished explaining my mother's recurring dream was that their story would make a great book.

After breakfast the four of us headed in multiple directions. Ian needed a few uninterrupted hours to write his weekly column and Luke decided to visit his office and the courthouse for the afternoon. Evidently, my step-dad, Agent Luke Myers, is responsible for establishing the FBI Child Protective task force that finally gained entry into that terrible foster home. As he hugged my mother good-bye I heard him say the kids were at the station giving their statements this morning, and he wanted to be there. Mom and I want to spend the afternoon at the mall picking up a few necessities for Scott and Brandon's new family. Evidently before leaving the party last night, my Mom, Mia and Julia created a shopping list – and split it three ways. We get to buy for baby Isabella. That child will want for nothing.

Twenty-four hours ago Ian and I thought our sole purpose this weekend was to shower my mother with love and give her spirits a lift. Instead we witnessed lives being saved and the birth of a family. Mission accomplished – my mother's spirits are definitely lifted. In fact all of us are sporting a silly grin today. And Ian's column? Completely brilliant – just as I knew it would be. The last few lines cause me to look toward the heavens and whisper a little thank you. This is not the end of our story, but a beautiful beginning of our forever.

Last night I witnessed a miracle. I watched two men, recently married, welcome three children into their family. Three children who before last night were forced to live in fear and filth. But this morning they're now part of a family. An extended, blended group of men and women who have pieced together an incredible, loving family. Few are connected by blood. Most are simply connected by love. It was my privilege to watch this story unfold.

This morning I heard a love story over breakfast – an honest-to-God, miraculous, connected through time love story. This couple makes marriage look easy, and love each other selflessly and completely every single day. Both events touched my heart beyond explanation.

My mother always told me family is what happens when two people fall in love . . . and I am in love with Grace. I'm happy to report that I am in fact loved by Grace and her family as well.

Family isn't always about blood – it's simply about connections with people. My family is full of people, young and old, who have touched my heart, accept me for who I am, make me hungry for life, and nourish my soul.

Every family has a story. Welcome to ours.

ABOUT THE AUTHOR

B.A. Dillon is a devoted wife and mother of two grown children, and a dedicated middle school math teacher. In addition to the Time Series, Dillon also writes a column, *Turn the Page*, for the monthly magazine 85 South, Out and About, published in the Atlanta area.

She lives in the Tampa area with her husband and two very spoiled dogs. Dillon has a slight obsession with Pinterest, music, words, books, and martinis!

With a Bachelors in Education and a Masters in School Counseling, Dillon has spent the last 26 years teaching a variety of subjects to middle school students. She hopes to retire in four years and concentrate on writing full-time.

BOOKS BY B.A. DILLON

THE TIME SERIES
(Romantic Suspense)
Tethered Through Time
A Vision in Time
It's About Time – a novella #2.5

Coming in 2016
Shattered by Time

58216476R00093

Made in the USA
Charleston, SC
07 July 2016